PRAISE FOR *AGATHA*

"Sharp, and, by turns, melancholy and wry . . . [A] nuanced and vivid story of a lonely young woman yearning for community and also yearning for everything she's had to give up to be part of that community." —Maureen Corrigan, NPR's *Fresh Air*

"Startlingly funny . . . Heartwarming without ever being saccharine . . . A person of any walk of life would enjoy reading *Agatha of Little Neon*." —Jenny Singer, *Glamour*

"Brilliant . . . [with] stunning, haunting prose." —Jackie Thomas-Kennedy, *Star Tribune* (Minneapolis)

"*Agatha of Little Neon* reaches that goal which all novels fundamentally pursue—saying something authentic and essential about the human experience—and does so with verisimilitude and the grace that comes with living simply." —D. W. White, *Chicago Review of Books*

"A smoldering, graceful debut." —Jenny Shank, *America*

"[A] deadpan novel about self-actualization, loss of faith, and the meanings of sisterhood." —Sophia June, *Nylon*

"Livel[y], funn[y] . . . Moving . . . *Agatha of Little Neon* is a novel of self-discovery and of faith." —Stephanie Zacharek, *Time*

"Subtle, sad, and beautiful . . . Crystalline minimalist prose [that] . . . evokes midcentury existentialist classics . . . This is the most moving book about grace and what it means to whisper a silent prayer to nobody that I read this year." —Ed Simon, *The Millions*

"I never knew I needed a book about four Catholic sisters reassigned to a neon-painted halfway house in a former mill town, but reader, I did." —Eliza Smith, *Literary Hub*

"Dynamic and resonant . . . . A lovely story of how cross-cultural exchange can foster hope."   —*Publishers Weekly*

"A charming and incisive debut."   —*Kirkus Reviews*

"*Agatha of Little Neon* is the rare kind of book that reads like a transmission from a person you don't know but who is already nestled close to your heart. Full of small devotions, pith and vigor, and a bounty of tender feeling for a world that is not quite as full of grace as it could be, this bold debut shines with a light all its own and announces Claire Luchette as a true original and a voice to follow closely."

—Alexandra Kleeman, author of
Something New Under the Sun

"There's not a false step in this novel of sisterhood, belonging, and what it means to choose a life for yourself. *Agatha of Little Neon* is a brilliant testament to Claire Luchette's skill and original voice."

—Lisa Ko, author of *The Leavers*

"Claire Luchette is so wildly talented that I would follow them anywhere. Here, it's to Woonsocket along with four women who are searching for meaning and a sense of belonging from one another and the world beyond. The result is a novel that's blazingly original, wry, and perfectly attuned to the oddness—and the profundity—of life."

—Cristina Henríquez, author of
The Book of Unknown Americans

"Claire Luchette is dazzlingly gifted, a master at balancing a sneaky deadpan wit with deep and genuine pathos. *Agatha of Little Neon* brilliantly mixes the sacred and the transgressive, the solemn and the absurd, and the profound, contradictory longings for belonging and independence. This book is a moving meditation on how to be a woman in the world—and how to be a human."

—Karen Thompson Walker, author of *The Dreamers*

Dotun Akintoye

CLAIRE LUCHETTE

AGATHA *of* LITTLE NEON

Claire Luchette has published work in the *Virginia Quarterly Review*, the *Kenyon Review*, *Ploughshares*, and *Granta*. A 2020 National Endowment for the Arts fellow, Luchette graduated from the University of Oregon MFA program and has received grants and scholarships from MacDowell, Yaddo, Millay Arts, Lighthouse Works, the Elizabeth George Foundation, and the James Merrill House. *Agatha of Little Neon* is Luchette's first novel.

AGATHA *of* LITTLE NEON

AGATHA *of* LITTLE NEON

CLAIRE LUCHETTE

PICADOR | FARRAR, STRAUS AND GIROUX | NEW YORK

Picador
120 Broadway, New York 10271

Printed in the United States of America
Originally published in 2021 by Farrar, Straus and Giroux
First paperback edition, 2022

The Library of Congress has cataloged the Farrar, Straus and Giroux
hardcover edition as follows:
Names: Luchette, Claire, 1991– author.
Title: Agatha of Little Neon / Claire Luchette.
Description: First edition. | New York : Farrar, Straus and Giroux,
2021.
Identifiers: LCCN 2021008693 | ISBN 9780374265267 (hardcover)
Subjects: LCSH: Nuns—Fiction. | Halfway houses—Fiction. |
Female friendship—Fiction.
Classification: LCC PS3612.U25525 A72 2021 | DDC 813/.6—dc23
LC record available at https://lccn.loc.gov/2021008693

Paperback ISBN: 978-1-250-84920-5

Designed by Gretchen Achilles

Our books may be purchased in bulk for promotional, educational, or
business use. Please contact your local bookseller or the Macmillan Corporate
and Premium Sales Department at 1-800-221-7945, extension 5442, or by
email at MacmillanSpecialMarkets@macmillan.com.

Picador® is a U.S. registered trademark and is used by Macmillan Publishing
Group, LLC, under license from Pan Books Limited.

For book club information, please visit facebook.com/picadorbookclub or
email marketing@picadorusa.com.

picadorusa.com • instagram.com/picador
twitter.com/picadorusa • facebook.com/picadorusa

1 3 5 7 9 10 8 6 4 2

for Barbara O'Brien Luchette

Galaxies of women, there

doing penance for impetuousness

—ADRIENNE RICH

PART I

POVERTY

1.

Mother Roberta made the rules: no chewing gum, no bicycles, no tree nuts, no pets. Every morning she brewed the coffee and every night she cooked the meal. Twice a year she sewed our made-to-measure habits from yards of a black poly-wool blend. She embroidered pillows, made punch from powder, wrote the homilies for the priest.

When Father Thaddeus came to Lackawanna, he suggested she might take a break. Relax. She was eighty-one, frail as filament, and had started having bad days. Lapses in memory, slips in the shower. She sometimes peed herself. Twice in one month, we'd had to rummage through bags of trash in search of her false teeth.

Mother Roberta acquiesced—she would try to relax. She began to spend her days behind a newspaper held wide, or at the kitchen table with a cup of Red Rose tea, staring at a spread of puzzle pieces that she never seemed to touch. But while we weren't looking, she put all thousand pieces where they were meant to be, and one afternoon the puzzle was finished. A moonscape. She left it on the table until dinner, then wrecked it and started again.

Everything we knew about living, we knew because Mother Roberta had showed us. She taught us to be busy: write our representatives, make bread of brown bananas. "There is no time for nothing," she used to tell us, when she caught us staring out the window, or flipping through stations on the rectory radio.

Mother Roberta had three stiff hairs on her chin that we

could spot only when she sat underneath the kitchen light. We used to fight each other for the chance to lean close and tug them loose. The thrill of it—we were eager, and she obliged, knowing she was too blind to get them herself. One of us would crouch and raise a pair of tweezers and, when a hair was plucked free, present it in front of Mother Roberta's face, so she could close her eyes, make a wish, and blow.

It seemed impossible then, in the time before Little Neon and Woonsocket, to imagine chin hairs of our own. The four of us were born in different months of the same year, each of us twenty when we became novitiates, twenty-two when we made our vows. We were twenty-nine when we moved from Lackawanna, just south of Buffalo, to Woonsocket. Back then, our chins were bald, our minds sharp. Our faith was firm and founded. We were fixed to one another, like parts of some strange, asymmetrical body: Frances was the mouth; Mary Lucille, the heart; Therese, the legs. And I, Agatha, the eyes.

There were a lot of parts missing, I suppose. But for a while we didn't realize it. For a while it seemed like enough.

When I was young, I thought womanhood would bring autonomy. Glamour. Fur coats and fat wallets. Days entirely of my design. I planned, as a girl, to become the kind of woman who kept a pen in her breast pocket; it seemed important that when I grew up I always had my own pen, that I never had to borrow anything from anyone else.

Now that I'm on my own, the thing I miss most is time spent in a parked van with my sisters, waiting for one of us to root through her bag and find whatever it was the other needed the most.

2.

Our ninth spring in Lackawanna, we painted the convent walls the color of mayonnaise.

This was in 2005, when newscasters couldn't stop talking about the death of the pope, and we couldn't stop talking about the mold on our bathroom wall. Remediation—that was the word we used. We wanted mold remediation. We bleached and squeegeed and scrubbed, but nothing worked. Nothing remediated. After a while we decided we might as well cover it up, which took three coats of what we agreed was the perfect white paint: not too yellow, not too blue. And then we painted the walls of the kitchen and the pantry and the foyer and the living room of our gable-front house. We kept painting until we ran out of walls.

It was the spring the babies stopped coming, so we had time on our hands. There used to be a dozen babies in our day care, some young enough that the mothers still counted their ages in months, others old enough to tell us how they felt. But a few years back a new Montessori school opened, and their budget allotted a music program, cooler toys, zoo-to-you animal visits—rabbits and turtles, mostly, maybe an iguana—and in the last few years, the mothers had started an enrollment exodus. Each year we had fewer babies. By our ninth spring, there was only one baby, and we thought four to one was an excellent teacher-to-student ratio, but the baby's mother felt it important for him to socialize. So then there were none. Not a single baby.

We stayed busy. We pruned the hedges and shampooed the

carpets. We were in possession of an old red Mercury Villager, a donation from a parishioner a few years back. The van had no air-conditioning. The seats were gray velour and the sliding doors were trouble; they jammed in their tracks. More than once we drove down the highway with the doors stuck halfway open, wind whipping through the car.

We couldn't fix the doors, but we could change the motor oil. Or—Therese could, while the rest of us watched. Only Therese was game and limber enough.

That spring, when Frances and Mary Lucille and I were standing around, eating corn chips, and Therese was belly-up under the car, Mother Roberta came outside barefoot to tell us the Buffalo diocese was kicking us out.

Mary Lucille put a chip in her mouth.

"I didn't catch that," Therese called from under the car. She stopped cranking her wrench. "What'd you say?"

"They're kicking us out," Frances said.

"What?"

Mother Roberta stooped to yell in the direction of Therese's head. "You're being reassigned! The Buffalo diocese is broke!" And when Therese said nothing, she yelled again, her face beet red. "Broke! Bust! In arrears!" Then she stood straight and turned to hock a fat loogie into the grass. She did not care to repeat herself.

There was silence, then the sound of oil hitting the pan. Therese let it all drip out, and then she tightened the bolt, emerged, wiped her blackened hands on a rag, and looked up at Mother Roberta. "How come?"

Mother Roberta reminded us about the decline in church attendance. The first year Father Thaddeus came to Lackawanna, the diocese's numbers had fallen by nearly half. This meant the offertory revenue dropped, too. The numbers fell the next year, too, and when they fell the year after that, we were sure they couldn't fall again.

They fell again.

Frances crossed her arms. "But can't we do something? We could sell muffins, or CDs, or—knives. I have a cousin who got rich from knives."

"Where would we get knives?" Therese asked.

"I can call my cousin," Frances said.

"No," Mother Roberta said, weary. She shook her head. "We are not selling knives."

"We could do a phone-a-thon," Mary Lucille said. "Ask people for donations."

"That's a nice idea," Mother Roberta said, "but it's too late for that. This is bankruptcy. Do you understand? This is huge debt. Colossal."

"But how?" Mary Lucille said. "We don't have any expensive things."

"Well," Frances said, "I've heard stories." A look of rapture came over her; she delighted in other people's secrets. "Someone in Williamsville told me that Father Art has had seven cosmetic surgeries."

"I thought so!" Therese said.

"Yeah. Neck lift, face lift, eye lift. Chin implants, too."

Mary Lucille's hand went instinctively to her own chin.

"And this other parish in Hamburg replaced all their bronze bells," she said. They opted for new bells that could ring themselves. Frances had heard they'd selected the most state-of-the-art operating system, Apollo. With Apollo, you could make the bells play any of the 7,800 songs from a customized digital library. The Apollo package came with a five-year warranty, a money-back guarantee, free annual maintenance, and a remote control.

7

So the men in charge had been reckless. "But come on," Therese said. "That's not enough to make the diocese go broke."

"Stop it. Just stop it," Mother Roberta said. She had no patience for gossip. "There's no sense trying to do the math." She hocked another loogie just past her feet.

It was Mother Roberta who kept the books for our parish. She knew where every penny went. She counted the offertory, paid the snowplow man, filed each grocery receipt. At the kitchen table she'd punch the calculator keys and fill the lines of the ledger, and it seemed to bring her joy.

Mother Roberta told us we had no reason to worry. "Reassignments happen all the time," she said. We knew this was true, but still we looked at each other with panic.

Mother Roberta said she would see to it that we were sent somewhere good. And together—we would be together.

Mary Lucille said, "But what about you?"

"It's time for me to retire," Mother Roberta said. "I'm not what I used to be. Time to go live with people my own age." Over in Batavia there was a home for elderly sisters, she told us. She'd be fine, she said. But I could tell she was vexed from the set of her jaw.

The five of us stood on the driveway, squinting in the sun. When there didn't seem to be anything else to say, Therese stood and uncapped the jug of motor oil. The rest of us watched her pour it into the engine.

3.

Mother Roberta was practiced at doing away with her anger. She did not cry. She did not yell. Instead, she'd scowl, mutter "Son of a pup," and hock a loogie. I'd watch her draw up from deep in her throat and sink one into a hankie, or far off into the grass, and I saw that for a moment she was set free from whatever had taken hold of her.

But sometimes the spitting wasn't enough. Sometimes dishes shattered. She would say, "I lost my grip," and I would nod and bring a broom. One time, she hung up the phone so hard the receiver cracked in half. Another time, I found her standing in front of the kitchen sink, where she'd lit a section of the newspaper on fire. "What're you doing," I said. She waited for the flames to die before she switched on the faucet and told me she was just cleaning up.

There were many days like that, days when I knew to stay out of Mother Roberta's way.

But there were other days when she wanted us close, when she'd call us to the kitchen to help her peel potatoes or pull the husks from corn or tell her a story while she alphabetized the spices. And those are the days I like to remember.

I can still see that version of us, younger and more at ease, returning from some errand, ambling down the grassy hill toward home. The sun pours down and makes parts of the road seem to shine, and we are buoyant, pink-cheeked, walking four across. The wind lifts our veils as we pick up speed, and we rush past trees made to droop by the weight of some forgotten snow. Our whole world waits for us at the bottom of the

9

hill, and we start to run, desperate to reach the driveway's end, where, through the kitchen window, we can see the face of Mother Roberta. She glances up from whatever task has kept her busy. Her face is expectant, lit up with love. And even now, years on, I can hear her voice: "Oh, they're back!" she cries. "They're back!"

4.

I've lost track of all the things we couldn't keep.

When there were still babies to look after, their mothers brought us gifts: nougat candy and good red wine and blown-glass ornaments. One afternoon, a box of frozen T-bone steaks, individually wrapped. After a baptism, we were given a basket of fragile fruit: soft pears, chunks of pale pineapple on sticks. After a funeral, Mother Roberta was once handed a hundred-dollar bill. This, she tucked in her habit to give to the rectory. The other things, we gave away—the miscellanea to the thrift, and the perishables to the food bank.

This wasn't always easy; we were tempted by the steaks.

Mother Roberta refashioned our future in one afternoon. She called a sister she knew in Albany, who talked to her mother superior, who passed along the phone number of a deacon in Hartford, who put her in touch with a vicar in Boston, who told her his archdiocese was strapped for cash, too, but he knew a woman religious who might be able to help. Abbess Paracleta headed an order that ran a halfway house called Little Neon, in a town in Rhode Island called Woonsocket.

Little Neon needed help. The live-in counselor had quit a couple of weeks before, and Abbess Paracleta had been filling in while she tried to find a replacement. She was looking for someone to keep people out of trouble. Ideally someone with experience, Abbess Paracleta said, but maybe one of us would do. "What about all four of them?" Mother Roberta said, and

Abbess Paracleta said if we didn't mind sharing the attic, she didn't see why not.

We didn't know much about addiction, about homelessness, but we knew how it could look. We'd watched a man nod into his own lap in the Tim Hortons on Abbott Street, had seen kids hawk lone red and white carnations in plastic sleeves to drivers on the interchange off-ramp. We'd heard the spellbound murmurs of the woman who sat all day at the bus shelter on Fillmore. We offered these people things we thought they'd want. Some days one said yes to a cheeseburger or a Filet-O-Fish or a hot coffee, and other days no one wanted anything but whatever coins and cash we had.

We were many times not helpful at all. One winter, Mary Lucille came across a man asleep next to the grocery carts in the Tops lot. She tapped him on the shoulder and asked, when he roused, if he wanted a ride to the shelter. He shook his head. Or, she said, she could take him to McDonald's for a chicken sandwich, or fries, or a parfait.

"A parfait?" the man said. He squinted at her. "What the hell is a parfait?"

We knew next to nothing about halfway houses and reentry and parole, but we knew how to look for information on the parish's hoary, cube-like computer. On the screen we read that Little Neon was formally called "St. Gertrude's Home for Transitional Living." The house used to be a convent, but a few years before, there had no longer been enough sisters to fill the beds, so Abbess Paracleta painted the house lime green and turned it into low-income housing for recovering addicts and ex-convicts—people who were trying to begin again. A person could stay in the house as long as they needed, provided they follow the rules. On the bottom of the main page, the site paraphrased 1 Corinthians: "God won't let you be tried beyond your strength." And, more mysteriously, Proverbs: "Can a man walk on hot coals without his feet being scorched?"

Frances said, "It sounds—"

"Hard," Mary Lucille said.

"No," Frances said, "incredible." She started to pace around the room, eyes cast low, lower lip in her teeth. "What could be more important than—than feeding the hungry, and sheltering the homeless, and comforting the sick!" She seemed taken with her own thoughts. "I was getting tired of babies, anyway. Honestly, I was kind of glad when they stopped coming. What can you even do with a baby?"

"You can sing to a baby," Mary Lucille said, her round face dreamy. "And you can watch a baby fall asleep in your arms. And do you remember when little baby Bruce would laugh? He'd get all riled up about something, and he'd scream his head off, and he'd thrash in your arms, kick you, claw at you, his face purple, snot everywhere, and it seemed like it would never end, the screaming! But then you'd rock him and get to work making him happy—and he'd hiccup and go quiet and look at you with those big eyes, and then when he giggled, it was like—oh—"

"It was a rhetorical question," Therese said. Mary Lucille looked at her hands.

"Anyway," Frances said. "I think it'll be good for us."

"Isn't the rate of recidivism really high?" Therese said. "I don't want anyone to recidivize on our watch."

"You mean recede," Mary Lucille said.

"No, I think it's—recidify," Frances said. "Or recidivate."

"Whatever," Therese said. "I don't want anyone going back to jail."

"Or relapsing," Frances said. "If they're just addicts, trying to get clean."

"Don't say 'just' addicts," Therese said. "And don't say 'clean.'"

"Don't even say 'addicts,'" Mary Lucille added. "Say 'a person with a drug habit.'"

"But that makes it sound like it's a matter of will," Frances said.

"'People with substance use disorders,'" Therese said, "is what's on the website." She pointed to the screen and pressed so hard the colors dimpled and bruised.

I wasn't sure if Rhode Island was an actual island, but I didn't want to admit this out loud, so later I sat alone in front of the computer and found a map showing its craggy edges. The Atlantic shoved its way in and crumbled the outermost corner of the state into a bunch of bitty islands. But most of the state was still attached to the rest of the country. Woonsocket was up top, near other towns that sounded mean: Cranston, Seekonk, Wrentham. I learned the state bird: the Rhode Island Red chicken. State tree: the red maple. State slogan: "Unwind." State motto: "Hope."

I also learned Rhode Island was where, earlier that year, a gay boy was dragged into the woods by his ankles and stabbed seven times in the neck. He was two weeks shy of sixteen. A birder found him belly-up in the pine needles, his throat split all over.

"They need you all the more, then," Mother Roberta said, when I told her. I wasn't sure who she meant by "they": gay people, or the ones who hated them. I didn't ask. I was afraid to know the answer, but now I think it was probably both.

I don't remember whom we prayed for that night. I don't remember which rosary we prayed—the sorrowful, maybe, or was it the glorious? But I do remember this: It was nice. It was easy. There was joy in being on my knees with the others, our spines straight, jaws lifting and dropping in unison. We were in the front pew of the basilica, strings of crystal rosary beads in our hands, and we moved our thumbs and forefingers in time along the beads. We did not rush, did not mutter, did not once open our eyes. And it wouldn't matter if we had, because there was nothing for us to see that we hadn't seen. We knew every inch of the church, had learned each mahogany pew and marble column and pane of candy-colored glass. That church! That nave! We had spent so many moments with our heads jerked back, learning the ceiling by heart: all those luminous painted scenes of heaven. Within the dome, a flock of seraphim carries Mary to God, while the twelve apostles look on from earth. We'd memorized the details, the exact color of the clouds, the eagle next to John, the palm tree behind Luke.

There was nothing new for us in that basilica, only things that had always been there, and though we could not admit it to each other, that's what we wanted, too: to always be there, in the place we'd become sisters. Remain, remain, remain.

5.

The Vatican elected a new pope our last month in Lackawanna. That day, we were all on our period. Mary Lucille's came first, in the night, a round blot on her sheets. The rest of us were bleeding by midmorning.

We should have been studied. As novitiates, we'd been shy, then giddy, when we found at the washing machine that all our full-cut briefs were stiff with blood on the same day. Ovarian synchrony! It was like a little miracle. It was like falling in love.

Mary Lucille announced that we'd run out of the thick pads we liked. For the thick pads, we had to drive to the bulk store four miles away. To drive to the bulk store, we needed keys to the van. For keys to the van, we had to go to Father Thaddeus in the rectory.

He was in the den, watching the news. On the screen, smoke plumed from the chimney of the Sistine Chapel. The newscaster said, "It's hard to say whether this is white smoke or black—I gotta tell you, Doug, it looks gray to me."

When we'd listened to the radio during breakfast, there'd been black smoke, which meant no consensus, but now there was smoke of an indeterminate color, which meant no consensus about the consensus. We wanted it to be white smoke, which would mean there was an answer. An end. We were tired of hearing Father Thaddeus talk about it. At meals he spoke with his mouth full, repeated himself, talked over us, explained things we already knew. He was obsessed, deeply invested. Therese suspected he'd put money on the outcome, but Frances didn't think so. She thought he suffered from dissociation. Frances liked to name other people's problems.

We stood in the doorway and Frances said hello, but Father Thaddeus didn't seem to register us. He was bent over, elbows on knees, as if he were watching an overtime quarter of football. He muttered, "Oh, for the love of Mike. How about that."

At forty-two, Father Thaddeus was exactly half the age of the deceased pastor, Father Doug. Fat Father Doug had had a massive heart attack one morning during a baptism. A baby in one hand, he clutched his chest with the other. The baby's wails were still echoing in the basilica when the paramedics lifted Father Doug into an ambulance. When we buried him, we knew that we would miss his generous laughter and his Sunday French toast, but we were surprised by how much we longed to hear him hum in the other room.

Father Thaddeus did not hum. He shrugged. He sighed and muttered and groaned. He ate sliced roast beef and fistfuls of spicy snack mix. His patience was cursory at best. In Mass, his homilies were brief and conversational, and he sped through Communion, doling out wafers in rapid succession—"Bodyof-ChristBodyofChristBodyofChrist."

But for the papal conclave, he seemed to have endless patience. He nodded when the newscaster said, "The whole world is waiting to be told the color of this smoke."

Frances cleared her throat. "Father, we'd like to use the car."

He did not turn from the screen. "What for."

"An errand," Frances said.

"What kind," he said.

To us, Frances rolled her eyes. To him: "It's personal. Lady stuff."

There was a pause. He was still staring at the smoke. "Key's on the hook," he said.

We were already out the door by the time he called, "Wait." We turned. He said, "Be back by dinner."

6.

Behind the wheel, Therese was agog, late to brake and quick to go. She took every yellow light and a number of reds. Frances sat shotgun, one hand tight on the over-door handle. In the back, Mary Lucille ate graham crackers for carsickness, and I pressed my forehead to the glass.

Everything was colored with the fact of our leaving, and the trip to the bulk store seemed then a valedictory drive through Lackawanna, a passing farewell to the junkyards full of car parts and the driveways of people whose daughters lay out, legs bare and gleaming. We passed the halal butcher and the non-halal butcher and the Dairy Queen.

Lackawanna. The town was built on iron ore by iron-willed people, and we'd survived nine ruthless winters there, hidden away in our little clapboard house.

"Hard to believe the next time we menstruate, we'll be in Rhode Island," Mary Lucille said, and sighed.

Outside the Lackawanna bulk store, there was a miniature steel horse that, for a dime, would swing you forward and back. Also, the entirety of a man's genitalia graffitied on brick.

Inside, we found a pyramid of cereal boxes. A love song playing overhead. Frilly greens, slick with mist. Melon, balled and chilled. Cellophane-wrapped roses and daisies dyed blue.

We put the maxi pads in our basket, and when we saw

nylons were on special, we sprung for those, too. They came folded inside paper cubes, showcased under little plastic windows.

After we paid, a boy carried our bag to our car, even though the pads and the nylons together weighed less than a loaf of bread. It was his job, he said. They'd had too many people stealing carts, or walking off with the potted begonias from the display out front. "Not that you would do that," the boy said.

"Oh, I'm not so sure," Therese said. "We have a bad reputation." The boy didn't see she was kidding, because he must not have known sisters could kid.

On the way home we were quiet. Frances turned on the radio, then switched it off just as quick. When Therese merged onto the thruway, we rolled the windows down, and the wind was so wild we could not speak.

A few miles out, just before our turn, the car issued a pained squeal; then, a snap. "I can't steer!" Therese cried, and we looked: the steering wheel was stuck, unyielding. "I can't steer!" she cried again, and started to brake. In the back Mary Lucille grabbed my hand, and we watched Frances fling herself over to help Therese force the wheel to the right. On the shoulder, Therese threw the gearshift into park and turned off the ignition, her chest heaving. For a moment, the four of us neither spoke nor moved.

Then Therese reached below the steering wheel and released the hood latch. We watched her step out to go stare at the engine's innards. And then, all at once, the three of us unbuckled and climbed out to join her.

With her bare hands, Therese checked the coolant and the transmission fluid. She'd tried, in the past, to teach us the parts of the engine: the alternator, the fuse box, the radiator, the spark plugs. But I retained nothing. When I looked at the engine, all I saw was places for trouble to hide.

Mary Lucille walked circles around the vehicle while Frances read aloud from the manual. Therese wriggled her way under the car and then wriggled her way free.

"I'm stumped," she said.

In the glove compartment there was a slim rectangular phone. Therese wiped her hands on her skirt and flipped it open, and it took a minute to hum to life.

She left a message. "Hi, Father, it's me, Therese. It's Friday evening, just about five p.m. Uh, so, we might be late for dinner. We're on Route Sixty-Two, mile marker eighty-two, and—do you know what it means when the steering wheel won't turn? Because ours won't turn. I can't figure it out. Okay, so, if you get this, call us back. The number's on the fridge."

Each time a car whipped past us, the van shook hard.

Therese called again, and when Father Thaddeus still didn't answer, she hung up. Mary Lucille said, "Maybe we should pray."

Therese gave her a look, then tossed the phone onto the front seat and went back to sink her arms into the depths of the engine.

If you look long enough, there is always something to blame.

Therese found the trouble: the serpentine belt—the black strap that moves the water pump—had snapped right in half. She pulled it free, a squirming length of rubber, and dangled it in the air for us to see. "Look," she said. She tucked it in a cup holder. With a bit of glue, she said, it would seal the gap under the convent's front door.

It was our belief that everything could become something else. Mother Roberta had showed us how to make bar soap from lye, how to keep out ants with cayenne pepper. We cleaned under our nails with the corners of offertory

21

envelopes. There's always a way to give something new life, but most people don't realize this. Most people don't want to know all the lives contained within disposable things.

"Now what?" Frances said.

"The nylons," I said. Everyone turned to look at me. "We could—well. Tie them."

A silence.

"And make a loop," Therese supplied. "Genius."

There was some debate as to whether we ought to use the old nylons we were wearing or the ones we'd just bought, which might be more durable, since they had no holes and windows. But we decided it was a shame to dirty brand-new ones, so we reached up our skirts and hopped on one foot, then the other, to kick our nylons free.

We watched Therese tie the feet to the waists and make a loop, and when she leaned into the engine to guide the nylons over the engine's pulleys, I bent to watch that, too. There was slack, so she tied the loop tighter. Her fingers caught grease and her forehead went slick with sweat and I held my breath. Therese told Frances to climb inside the driver's seat, and she gave her a signal, and the engine turned over and we watched the pulleys spin, and the nylon moved the disparate parts at a speed I could only guess at, and when Frances moved the steering wheel, the tires moved, too. We whooped. We hollered. We laughed. Amid the thick fields, along the broad paved road, we had found a way to move.

While we were threading hosiery through the car engine, Father Thaddeus called to say he was coming to save us. The voicemail was panicked, as if it were he who was in trouble.

Frances tried to call him again to say we didn't need help, but he didn't pick up.

We could have made it all the way home that way, we were sure, nylons holding the car together. But many times, the greatest mercy you can grant a man is the chance to believe himself the hero. This was obedience, we thought.

And so Frances snapped the phone shut and Therese slipped the loop of nylons from the pulleys. She slackened the knots, and we wordlessly tried to distinguish them. Frances and I were the same size, and our pairs had the same reinforced toes, but hers were tawnier. Therese was tallest, and spindliest, and needed the longest, palest pair. Mary Lucille needed the widest waist and shortest legs.

When she'd hiked hers up, Therese bent to put the serpentine belt where she'd found it, and then she slammed the hood shut.

Back in the van, we folded our dirty hands and waited for Father to arrive. We sang low hymns and watched the grass take the wind. We waited. We whistled. We counted the cars that passed.

The parish florist gave Father Thaddeus a ride to mile marker 82. We could see, from where we were parked on the roadside, the pale faces of the men in the purple van, perched among the florist's bouquets. Lilies pressed up against the windows, ranunculi in the passenger seat, and the waxen face of our parish pastor above his white collar.

"Oh dear," Father said, when he stepped out of the van. "What did you do?"

We popped the hood and let him look. Father shoved his shirtsleeves high, frowned into the depths, and we stood behind him, arms crossed. He muttered to himself; we did not

23

say a word. Even though we could point to the problem, knew what the van needed, we stood and let the wind upset our veils, and we waited while he stared at the valves and hot pistons, allowing him the time he needed to conclude whatever he would.

7.

Maybe it was lily-livered, the way I watched it all happen, never dared object to the way things were.

Over the next few weeks, the convent sold our every armchair, every last fork and knife. From the kitchen window I watched people walk off with all our stuff. One man gave Mother Roberta seventy-five cents for the Ping-Pong table, and then, when the table was too big for his truck, he asked for his quarters back. We gave away crates full of beat-up toys and picture books. All three space heaters, the davenport, the window blinds, the bottle of bleach—every day, more things left. And then, one morning in the middle of May, the time came for us to leave, too.

It was still dark when we said goodbye to Mother Roberta on the driveway. She was in her nightgown and slippers, and her hair stuck straight up on one side. She handed each of us a Slim Jim and an apple and a bar of lavender soap.

Mary Lucille was crying. Then we all were.

"Pick seats in the middle of the bus," Mother Roberta said. "It's safest in the middle. Everyone always thinks the front is safest, but if you're in the front when there's a head-on collision—" She made a low whistle. "And wear your seat belts. And be kind to the driver." Then she hugged us, there on the driveway in the early morning dark.

When it was my turn to be hugged, I didn't know how to let go of Mother Roberta. After a moment she kissed my cheek and pulled away.

"Get going," she said.

So we left for the bus depot, walking single file down the driveway and along the side of the road. We'd packed light: sheets, nightgowns, underwear, sunscreen. As we went, our duffel bags thudded against our legs.

A few days later, Mother Roberta would leave, too. Father Thaddeus drove her to the home for elderly sisters in Batavia, where everyone lived on the first floor and she wouldn't have to wash the dishes. I wondered if she'd have preferred to live out her days where she'd always lived them, in Lackawanna. One of our last nights together, I asked her if she was sad to leave. "God is calling me there," she said, just like God was calling us to Woonsocket. But the way she said it, it sounded like "Quit whining." It sounded like "Grow up." She'd been eating Hershey's Kisses, and I watched her crush the foils in her fist.

It was impossible for me to tell just from looking, as we walked to the bus depot, whether the others were, like me, afraid to leave, or if they were so somber with a sense of obligation that they never let themselves feel dread. Perhaps they were determined to love whatever awaited us and expected nothing else. I watched them walk ahead, their heads bent low, habits fluttering, and couldn't make up my mind how they felt.

How wonderful it would be, to wring yourself of questions.

At the bottom of the hill, I turned back to look at our little house. Mother Roberta had gone inside the garage, and it looked like she was waving to us, but then the garage door shut. She'd been reaching for the handle.

8.

Woonsocket: a tuckered-out town in northern Rhode Island, split down the middle by a river of waste. The sidewalks were littered with condoms and crushed empties. From Woonsocket you could vomit into Massachusetts; from Massachusetts, kids came to buy liquor and fentanyl after nine.

No bus would take us straight to Woonsocket; instead, we spent the morning on one Greyhound, that night on a second Greyhound, and the next morning on a third, our legs kinked up in the stiff-backed seats the whole way.

Woonsocket, Rhode Island: on the bus we repeated the syllables until they became discrete and strange. Rode Eye Land. Road Aye Lend. Roe Dial End.

We sat four across in the middle of the bus and whispered the rosary in the morning and at night, moving at fifty-five miles an hour. I want to think that no one on that bus looked sidelong at us as they passed down the narrow aisle, that it wasn't fear or contempt that made people avert their eyes and hold their children close as they walked past us. But I know better. Four sisters in heavy habits, muttering Glory Bes, who slept with their mouths open and ate beef jerky straight from the plastic. We were the opposite of invisible, but still difficult for people to see. When people saw our habits, they ceased to see our faces.

As a girl, as soon as I knew what prayer was for, I prayed for likeness. "Dear God," I said, every night. "Make me unexceptional." When hairdressers or dental hygienists called me pretty, or told me they liked my curly hair and my cola-colored eyes, it was clear I was supposed to be flattered. But flattery wasn't what I wanted. I wanted to be overlooked. To recede. The highest praise anyone could give me was that I looked just like another girl they knew, that they could have sworn we were twins.

And for a while, with my ordinary ponytail and the right blue jeans, I went unnoticed. I had no glasses or braces or birthmarks or special talents. Teachers sometimes forgot who I was and called me by some other girl's name. I loved this. I wanted to be indistinguishable.

I was eleven when my mother died. I missed four days of school, and when I returned, it seemed that I had, through no deed of my own, given everyone a reason to know my name. For many months, kids looked at me sidelong in the classroom. If they spoke to me, it was with both pity and dread. My homework, too, was looked at differently: spelling errors went uncounted, miscalculations uncorrected.

I was marked by grief. There was nowhere for me to disappear, except in the back of the church each week, when I'd sit alone and fold my hands and say the prayers I knew. The words were always in the same order, unchanged from when my mother was alive.

When I was young, I didn't speak; I recited. I pledged allegiance. I hailed Mary, full of grace. In the bath, I sang songs I'd heard on commercial breaks: songs about carpet cleaners, mint gum, Coca-Cola, cat food. My dolls spoke to each other about medication side effects and furniture closeout sales.

My mother had sent me to a school for kids who had trouble doing what other children could do with ease. I had an impediment, they said, and they assigned me an aide. No one could understand why I hated talking, why it was so much work to come up with something to say. It was even more work to make it true or funny or smart. And then when you'd come up with it, you had to say it, and live with having said it.

But after my mother died, I found things to say in church. On Sundays I could be anonymous. I found a little constancy: the familiar rhythm of the hour, the stories with endings I knew. I didn't have to come up with a way to be all right—I could just stand in line and wait for a priest to place Communion in my palm. Church explained nothing of my life, but church pulled me forward. I crossed myself and said amen and made my way down the aisle.

9.

The world outside the bus window disappeared. If I looked, I would have seen the shape of my face in the glass. The sturdy chin, my mother's straight nose. I might have been able, if I leaned close, to count the freckles on my cheeks, or point to the scar where I'd slipped on the diving board when I was seven. But I did not see any of this, because I did not like to look.

My mother had been dead eight years when I started selling scratch-off tickets and gallons of gasoline at a gas station outside of Buffalo. All the girls I'd known in high school were becoming nurses or wives, and I'd wanted to become neither. I worked the night shift. One heavy man came each evening to take home the same prepared foods: a roast beef sandwich on a kimmelweck roll, wrapped in white paper; loose grapes in a cup; two slices of cheesecake in separate plastic containers, varnished with bright cherries in syrup. Each night I asked the man if he needed a fork for the cheesecake, and each night he said he did. Even though I knew what his answer would be, I kept asking. I hoped he'd someday decide to reuse the fork from the day before, and I waited every night to see if he'd change.

My brother was twelve and learning algebra; I was nineteen and learning how to look people in the eye. I was learning other things, too: how to distinguish packs of cigarettes by color, the names of the blacks and yellows and reds. I was memorizing the refrain of every pop song on the radio. But mostly I was learning that the only way for the night to end is for the night to end. There was no way to speed up a lonely hour.

There must have been nights, back then, when I did not feel lonely or afraid, when I did not come home to my father's house and cry in the dark. But these are not the nights that I remember. Instead, there's just this: whole evenings spent with my elbows on the counter, staring out the wide window of the convenience store. I was looking into the cars parked at the pump; I was looking for other people. I wanted to see who stayed in the passenger seat while the driver filled the pump. Women, mostly. They looked at their faces in the overhead mirrors, or they smoked out the window, or they turned to calm a baby in the backseat.

In the morning I would go home and sit in the glow of my father's television, reruns set to mute, certain that there was nothing more wonderful than to know someone was sitting somewhere, waiting for you.

Sometimes people came into the store and sometimes they did not, and one night when the bell chimed I looked up to see a woman in a habit.

I'd known only one nun as a kid, the elderly woman who taught sixth-grade history. She was tetchy and quick to yell, and I thought that all nuns in existence were the same: unpleasant, mad at the world. When I was young, my mother took me to Mass, and on the drive home she made fun of the nuns. She said they had emotional problems and buck teeth, and she'd stick out her teeth in the rearview mirror, and I would laugh and laugh.

But this woman was different, many years younger and smiling. Buoyant: she looked buoyant. And this was unusual, because no one in South Buffalo looked buoyant. Everyone looked as if they'd already sunk.

The nun came for cough drops, which she paid for with quarters and dimes. I studied her face as she dropped the coins in my hand—it brought me calm.

"Cough?" I said.

"Beg pardon?"

"You have a cough?"

She said no, but one of her sisters did. She was on her way home from the county prison, over in Alden, and thought she'd stop.

"That's a long drive," I said.

She said she didn't mind it. "And we take turns driving. There's a few of us who go, serve communion." She tucked the cough drops in her purse.

She lingered near the sunglasses, displayed on a rotating tower near the rows of bagged nuts. I watched her spin the tower and select a pair of aviators, then bend to consider her face in the janky mirror. She wasn't satisfied, so she reached for others—I watched her try the chunky oversized ovals and the cat eyes and the wraparounds and the heart-shaped ones. And it was while she was looking at the world through the heart-shaped ones that another nun came into the gas station. "Well, if it isn't Lolita," the other nun said, and they both cracked up.

Later, I would learn how to tell this story. I would revise my own memory. I would describe, for those who asked, a version of the evening that involves my sudden understanding of the will of God. I have learned that people like to hear about callings. Vocations are half magic, half luck, reserved for the chosen few. But the truth is that I do not remember a call, not the way it happens in Scripture: sudden, unexpected, unmistakable. A vision, maybe, or the distinctive voice of God. An angel appearing in a dream.

I do believe there are women who hear their names and

wake with a start, but not me. There was no invitation. There was only that night in the gas station: it was late, and I was lonely, and I understood, watching the two nuns, that you could live your whole life alone if you weren't careful. You might never find a decent place to hide from yourself.

"What about these?" the first nun said, when she'd slipped on another pair of frames.

Her friend considered. "No, no. Here, try these." And she handed her a different pair.

10.

Somewhere outside of Albany, a woman with a young baby boarded the bus and chose a seat in front of Mary Lucille and me. She was around our age, this woman, and her child sounded displeased to be on a bus—not wailing yet, but about to. Mary Lucille leaned forward to say hi to the baby, her voice gooey and warm like it always was when she spoke to something small. "Hello, sweet girl," she said. "How old?" she asked the mother.

"Seventeen months last Tuesday," the woman said.

"Let me know if you'd like me to hold her for a while," she told the mother. "If you need a minute. A little break."

"Oh, wow, yeah," the mother said. "Please. Go ahead." And she handed the baby to Mary Lucille with obvious relief. "Her name's Judy."

"Judy!" Mary Lucille cooed. The baby went quiet, eyes wide. "You've got the cutest little cheeks! Yes you do!" She turned to show me the baby's face. "Agatha, doesn't she have the cutest little cheeks?"

"Yeah," I said, and turned to the window. Babies made me nervous. In Lackawanna, when there were still babies at the day care, I did what I could to avoid them. Frances and Mary Lucille and Therese were expert caregivers, competitive with their compassion. The three of them vied for the babies' love.

But it was Mary Lucille whom the little ones seemed to like best. Watching her lift a baby to her chest, you'd see something turn soft and loose inside her. She loved to burp them. She loved to feed them, soothe them, wipe them, change them.

Frances and Therese sometimes lost their patience, tucking spoons past their little lips again and again. But Mary Lucille was calm. She'd smile and lift a towel and keep going.

I preferred to watch. The mothers liked to know what went on during the day, so I walked around with a clipboard and kept track of crying jags and naps and diaper changes. Once Therese tried to show me how to change a diaper. You lay the baby belly-up on the table and unsnap its pants. Then you strip the diaper free, grab the ankles to lift, and work a wipe front to back. Therese made me use one hand to spread open a new diaper and the other to tape it shut, and then she showed me how to fold up the old one so nothing came loose. She was fast. She was thorough. I wasn't very good. I stuck to my clipboard after that.

Mother Roberta used to tell us what it was like when the day care first opened. In those days, Mother Roberta told us, religious orders were either changing too quickly or not changing quickly enough. There'd been talk, before Vatican II, that maybe the pope would decide to let women into the priesthood. He didn't. But he did allow sisters to engage more with the world. Uncloister themselves. Mother Roberta told us while women in other orders boarded buses to work with the poor, the Lackawanna order was slower to make progress. Everyone debated whether they'd wear long habits or short habits or no habits at all. They settled on long habits, and then they elected to open the day care. It was something, Mother Roberta said, but she'd have rather had holy orders.

On the bus, the baby fell asleep in Mary Lucille's arms, and in the seat ahead of us, the mother fell asleep, too.

11.

On the last leg of the trip, we passed a wind farm. A dozen towering turbines stuck in the ground on either side of the highway, gathering the power of the gales. "Look," I said, and the others glanced. The turbines stood lean and spare and silent. Stoic: that's what they were. Wind energy, I knew, was something good, but I hadn't pictured it so elegant. I liked that if I focused on the revolution of one blade, the operation appeared slower than if I considered all the blades together.

The final hour of the trip was unbearable. There was roadwork outside of Worcester, and the traffic was so bad it felt as if we moved one inch at a time. When we finally arrived in Providence, Abbess Paracleta was waiting in the parking lot, arms crossed as if we should have been sorry, should have done something to prevent the traffic.

There was so much of her. She was as tall as the cab of her flatbed truck, with jowls and square shoulders, and she wore the same black habit we did, but hers was thick wool, no blend. She hadn't quite rubbed in all the sunscreen she'd applied to her cheeks and forehead and nose, as if she'd been in a rush.

We said hello. We thanked her for coming. We presented her with a deck of playing cards we'd bought at a rest stop. On the back of each card was a full-color picture of Niagara Falls.

"What for," she said.

"For fun," Frances said.

In the truck Therese sat shotgun, her long legs up against the glove compartment. Frances and Mary Lucille took the back jump seats, and I sat on top of Mary Lucille. Her breath was sour and hot. We did not speak. Abbess Paracleta rushed the engine and charged onto the thruway, soaring past slower cars. Each bump made Mary Lucille wince under my weight. I watched the odometer needle drop to the right. The abbess drove in silence; she said nothing about the route or the weather or the roads. On the phone the week before, she had sounded excited about our arrival, but she now seemed stripped of enthusiasm, as if she had, upon seeing us in person, perceived and could not forgive our ineptitude.

We sped on to Woonsocket. Abbess Paracleta had described it, over the phone, as the sneeze between Boston and Providence. "There'll be so much wind you'll think the world will run out."

She had spent the past couple of weeks keeping watch over the five people who had come to live in Little Neon. "I can't tell you how much I'm looking forward to sleeping in my own bed again," she said now. "And getting back to my liturgical work. It's such a relief that you're here."

I watched the abbess reach for her handbag on the floor. Her foot heavy on the gas, she held the wheel with her knees and rummaged in her bag until she'd found what she wanted: a letter envelope. And from the envelope, I watched her remove translucent slices of pink ham, wet and limp.

She offered us some.

I shook my head.

"No, thank you," Frances said.

Therese said, "I'm all set, thanks."

Mary Lucille said, "Yes please," and the abbess dangled a slice for her to take. Mary Lucille folded the whole thing into her mouth. Therese made a face.

"I didn't have time to pack a real lunch," Abbess Paracleta said. "But I love ham. People don't realize that most meats will travel well," she said. "You can slip cured ham in an envelope, toss it in your handbag, and you'll find it later"—here she tore a slice and stuffed one half, then the other, into her mouth—"when you're crying in a phone booth, or when you're alone in the unlit stairwell of a damp parking garage." She swallowed, licked a thumb. "And you will rejoice."

Mary Lucille nodded, and I nodded, too. I could tell it meant something to the abbess, the ability to calm herself down. It's a skill I envied. I'd never learned, not for all the times I'd been alone and afraid, all the nights I'd worked the Sunoco counter, all the times a stranger paralyzed me with a lecherous look. Prayer could only protect a woman from so much.

Abbess Paracleta ate with one hand and steered with the other, and I counted the miles that passed. The land outside my window was the continuous kind of ground: sweeping sameness with no intervals, no ways of marking difference.

12.

Little Neon was the color of Mountain Dew. Abbess Paracleta told us later she'd bought the paint on clearance. You could see it from three streets away: a bright yellow-green narrow colonial smack dab in the middle of a sea of beige and gray colonials. White shutters, white door, black driveway, a white van parked in front of the bright green garage. It was like looking at the sun. All I could see, even when I blinked, was Little Neon green. It looked chemical, lurid and lovely at the same time.

"Are we here?" Mary Lucille said, when the abbess parked in the driveway.

"Duh," Frances said.

Tim Gary was the first person we met in Little Neon, the only one home when we arrived. I was careful not to stare. Before you're face-to-face with a man, you imagine he'll have all the bones that you do, more or less. But Tim Gary had only half a mandible. His face was lopsided: the right side dropped off just below the cheekbone, the skin puckered and shapeless and loose. When he spoke, the words came out muffled and flat. He was skinny, fragile-looking, with thin hair that was carefully parted and combed. His eyes were kind, the lashes long.

We unpacked our duffel bags in the attic of the home. The abbess had lined up four cots in a cramped row. I took the one by the window. That attic! It was never meant to be lived in. The door we couldn't lock, the floorboards that swelled and shrank, the vaulted ceiling so low we had to stoop. Even now,

I am transported there by the strangest things: a splinter; the smell of mothballs or medicated shampoo.

Tim Gary started to tell us how parts of his jaw were taken away. "You're probably wondering what happened to my face," he said.

Abbess Paracleta stabbed a broom at the corners of the attic and coughed at the dust. She said, "The sisters are tired from their trip, Tim Gary. Maybe you save the story."

But Tim Gary did not save the story. The others kept stuffing pillows into cases; I turned and looked at him as he spoke. He started and did not once stop. I watched him push out the words with evident effort. Like me, I thought, but jawless.

Two winters ago, he told us, he had a cancerous section of jaw removed, then another, then another. Then part of his tongue. If you were rich, he said, doctors could rebuild your jaw with a piece of bone from your leg. But he wasn't rich.

He had hurt; he had hungered. After the surgery, he was fed through a tube. And then his lips were numb for weeks after they pulled the tube out, so he subsisted on liquids. Green ice pops were better than orange; chicken broth was too salty and made him bloat.

That's when the trouble with pills started, he said. He learned to like Dilaudid more than he liked any living person or liquid meal. Now he was back to eating solid foods, and he'd given up pills, but his meals had to be soft and easy and slow. He brushed his teeth with a toothbrush made for a kid.

"And now all the cancer's gone, but so's five inches of my jawbone," he said.

Tim Gary had found good work as a fry cook. He had half a nursing degree and an ex-wife in Delaware, and maybe one day, he told us, he'd go back for both. He had no wife, or girl-friend, or lover, but Tim Gary had his habits. And, he told us, he wouldn't be changing them. Not for us, not for anyone. He worked late and woke late. He drank fat Pepsi and orange juice with calcium. He liked to pray but didn't like to be told what to pray for.

Abbess Paracleta dragged a finger through the grime on the window glass. "There's a chore wheel," she told us. "But you're going to have to remind them."

"Oh, we love to clean," Therese said, though this was only true of the three of them. I was the untidy one, the one who left dishes in the sink, who'd rather swallow a mop than push it across the floor.

Abbess Paracleta showed us around the house, listing rules as she went. She had more rules than Mother Roberta. No napping on the rust-colored corduroy couch in the front room. No TV after 10:00, and no hogging the remote. She showed us the collection of board games in the hall closet: no gambling, no foul play, and no dirty words or proper nouns in Scrabble.

The residents of Little Neon—Neons, she called them, so we would, too—slept on the second floor in shared rooms (no sex; no co-sleeping; no kissing; no hugs longer than three seconds; no holding hands). The rooms were spare and the beds narrow. There wasn't any clutter, save for balled-up socks in the front room and a comic book splayed open on the floor of the other. "The boys in the front room—Tim Gary and Pete and Baby. Jill and Horse out back," the abbess said. "You can move the beds around, if you have to. If someone leaves, and someone else comes in."

"Why would someone leave?" Mary Lucille asked.

"That's the whole point of being here: someday you leave.

When the time comes. When your parole's up. But no one's very close. Baby has another eight months. Pete has eleven."

Frances said, "And the others—"

"They're here to quit something. And once they're healthy enough, they leave,, too." She led us downstairs. "It's pretty simple. To live in Little Neon, all they have to do is keep their jobs and stay off drugs and follow all the rules. And in turn, I hope you'll try to show them that their lives aren't over, even if they've messed up," she said, and turned back to look at us. "Only dead is dead."

In the kitchen, there was a long dining table with a dozen mismatched chairs and an old white fridge (no energy drinks; no alcohol, obviously, and no drugs; no smoking on the property); the chore wheel (dishes, toilets, mop, vacuum, dust); the medicine cabinet (which was locked at all times; she whispered the code). Dinner was at 6:00 and curfew was 10:00 p.m. sharp, unless someone had to work third shift, but they could only work third shift with permission.

Sunday Mass was not required, but strongly encouraged. "Nonbelievers go for the donuts after," she said. Monday morning, we were to administer drug tests; we could also test at random and break out the Breathalyzer whenever we had reason to. Pee cups and test sticks were under the bathroom sink. No midriffs, no bikinis, no spandex, no cleavage, no razors, no candles, no guests.

On the fridge door was a list of phone numbers. "Parole officers and sponsors up top," Abbess Paracleta said. "Methadone clinic and parish contacts underneath."

"What's methadone?" Mary Lucille said.

"It's what they give you to help you quit opiates," Abbess Paracleta said.

"And opiates," Therese said, "are drugs derived from opium. Heroin, morphine, codeine—"

"I know what opiates are," Mary Lucille said.

Abbess Paracleta led us out the back door. On the edge of the driveway there was a low basketball hoop, the net gone threadbare, and a stiff green garden hose. And beyond that, a half acre of high grass left untended, a single oak tree in the middle.

We squinted in the sun. "Lots of room for a garden," Frances said. She knelt down and touched the soil. "Hardy greens would take just fine. And root vegetables. Unless there's no gardening allowed?"

"There can be gardening," Abbess Paracleta said. "That's not a bad idea."

I pointed at a white pine box. "What's that?"

"A beehive," she said. "Or, it used to be. The old bees did not winter well." We watched her walk over to the hive and open it up with her bare hands. No bees came out. She pulled free a rectangular sheet, like a file from a cabinet, and showed us the dozens of dead bee carcasses, stuck to the beeswax. "Tim Gary was the one who handled them. He loved the bees. Last winter he sealed the hive in plastic and poured in a pound of sugar," she told us, "which usually works to tide the bees over. But somehow snow and cold got in, and they all froze to death."

"Oh, that's terrible," Mary Lucille said. "Terribleterribleterrible."

Abbess Paracleta nodded and slipped the beeswax back in the hive.

"Can we play basketball?" Therese said. "I know how to change a net."

"Sure," the abbess said. "There can be basketball."

"What if we hung a bird feeder?" Mary Lucille said. "Just a small one, near the window. Would that be okay?"

"Why not. But I wouldn't put it near the house," Abbess Paracleta said, leaning on the beehive. "They'll crash into the glass. Better to hang it from the oak."

Mary Lucille said, "But then I won't be able to watch the birds."

"Well," Abbess Paracleta said, "that's not really the point, is it?"

She told us people used to come and unscrew the porch lights if they couldn't find any other scrap metal to sell, so she'd screwed a glass fixture around them. "Soda cans, I like to leave near the street, so whoever needs them doesn't have to walk up the drive and rifle through the trash," she said.

In Little Neon's driveway there was a wide white van. Not a minivan, like our old Mercury Villager, but a big, box-like thing. Church property. "Pete is the one who drives," the abbess said, standing in front of it. "With permission, of course. And supervision—one of you will have to go along every time he drives. Or you can drive, if you'd rather. It's tricky to park this thing, but he's good at it. Maybe he can teach you."

We all looked at Therese. She put a hand to the hood and smiled. "Oh yeah," she said. "I'd love to take this baby for a spin."

In the garage there was a filing cabinet where Abbess Paracleta kept alphabetized folders with information on every Neon. Medical histories, police reports, court paperwork, the abbess's handwritten notes on each person. "Anyone breaks a rule, or acts out, you have to write it down. Make sure there's a record. Just in case."

"Just in case what?" Frances asked.

"Just in case."

We were standing in the kitchen when two women came home. The first through the door was tall, even taller than Abbess Paracleta, and leaner, wearing a big purple parka and black leggings despite the heat, her thickish hair piled atop her head. "Most people call me Lawnmower Jill," she said, or L.J. for short, "on account of I drive a lawnmower everywhere." She couldn't drive a car because she had tried too often to drive a car while drunk.

The other woman stood no taller than five feet, and her hair was shorn close. She introduced herself as Horse. "Like the animal," she said. She wore work boots and canvas pants, and she'd sweated through the neck of her T-shirt. Acne scars marked the skin of her face.

"Why Horse?" Therese said.

"She can fall asleep standing up," Lawnmower Jill said.

"Also, the heroin," Horse said. She looked like she was twenty years older than us, but we found out later it was just a few years' difference.

"But her real name's Eleanor," Abbess Paracleta said. "What happened to Pete?"

"A meeting," Horse said. "With Baby."

"Pete works with Horse at the granite yard," the abbess told us. "Every day they go out and install new countertops for people. They do really beautiful work. You should see it. The yard has huge slabs of marble in pink and white, feldspar and

45

quartz, and it's just gorgeous when it's all finished and smooth and shining. And Jill—"

"I work at the convenience store," Lawnmower Jill said. "The Tedeschi. I make sure the chips get hung up right." She took off her parka and revealed a red vest, a name tag pinned near her armpit.

"How nice," Mary Lucille said. "What a blessing. It's wonderful that you have somewhere to go and something to do." She was quoting Mother Roberta. It's what Mother Roberta used to say a person needed in life: somewhere to go and something to do. She said it to give a person hope. But when Mary Lucille said it, it sounded like pity.

Lawnmower Jill just blinked. For a moment, no one said anything. Then Therese asked Lawnmower Jill what kind of mower she drove.

"A 1998 John Deere Bronco," she said. She turned and went upstairs until dinner.

Pete and Baby showed up in time to eat. Pete had a bald head and a red face, and he looked maybe fifty. And Baby was young, teenage, his face rosy with acne, limbs lanky and tattooed. He told us he worked at the ice factory.

"Ice," Frances said. "Like, cubes?"

"Yeah, cubes," he said.

"Just cubes?" Therese said.

"Blocks, too," Baby said.

"Neat," Mary Lucille said. "Or should I say—cool."

Therese groaned.

We crowded around the table, the abbess at the head. I chose a seat between Baby and Tim Gary.

For us, Abbess Paracleta had fried pork chops and boiled

potatoes and served peaches in halves. Poured room-temp birch bark soda straight, no ice. On the table, the food steamed, and I salivated while we waited to pray. Baby snuck a piece of potato and Horse slapped his hand.

For Tim Gary, Abbess Paracleta toasted bread and buttered it limp. She scrambled an egg and sliced a banana and stuck a straw in a glass of whole milk. She placed it before him, and he told her, before he tried his food, that what was in front of him was the best dinner he'd ever had.

And that's when Tim Gary started to cry. Tiny, pained gasps. He palmed fast at his cheeks and eyes.

Mary Lucille said, "What is it, Tim Gary?"

He said, "Oh, I just feel blessed, is all." He sipped his milk, and when some dribbled from his mouth, Abbess Paracleta lifted a napkin to his chin.

We reached to hold hands. Abbess Paracleta issued a prayer of gratitude and ended with the words "May God's work be done here in Woonsocket."

13.

After dinner, Tim Gary wanted to show us the wind turbines.

"Oh, they're beautiful," Pete said. "You have to see them. I can drive."

I thought this sounded like a nice idea, but I could see from my sisters' faces this was not what they wanted. They were tired from the trip. They looked like they wanted hot tea and to sleep until dawn. But they kept this to themselves.

"We have to make it brief," the abbess said. "I have to get back to Providence." So Pete fired up the white van. All of Little Neon went, and Abbess Paracleta, too. When we climbed in, Therese asked Pete, "What kind of engine we got in this thing?"

"V-eight," he said. "Three hundred horsepower."

Therese nodded with approval. "Listen to her purr!"

The van could sit fifteen. The four of us sat in the middle, though it occurred to me that maybe it was selfish to always take the safest seats. The seats were cracked plastic, the backs pimpled with chewed gum.

Pete drove through town with the unhurried calm of a confident man. He seemed to know every stop sign and pothole. We passed the fill station, where bright lights made the pumps seem to hover above the earth, and we went by a tavern, Nick's, but the first letter had burnt out, so it looked like ICK's. Blockbuster, credit union, methadone clinic, dollar store, payday loans, the Tedeschi with a special on two-liters of pop ("There's where the Lord's called me to work," Lawnmower Jill said when we passed). The bus lurched over the Blackstone River, which looked like sludge in the night. Then we got to gliding on Cumberland Street.

Outside the bus, I stood, stunned.

The turbines surrounded us, but all we could see were their tiny red lights that blinked against the black night. Warning signs in excess. The lights flashed, steady and in synchrony, and I spun to see them, to confirm that yes, the turbines behind me blinked with the turbines before me. The red lights stretched forever, dim off in the distance and severe near the road.

These were the same windmills I had seen from the Greyhound. They'd seemed proud in daytime, but in the dark they struck me as anxious. Afraid.

Tim Gary said, "Let's go look up close."

We followed him single file through damp grass. Baby stopped to look at something that clung to his shoe. Mary Lucille stopped, too, and shrieked to identify, when she bent over to see, the wet, limp body of a fallen bat.

"Bat!" she cried. "Bat! Bat! Batbatbatbatbatbatbatbatbat!"

"Calm down," Lawnmower Jill said. "It's just a bat."

Tim Gary went and looked. He said, "Some days, there's hundreds of them."

Up close, the turbines were fat and serene as ships. The whir was like passing traffic. I knocked the metal to hear the hollow ring. The wind rushed at me as I walked circles around the giant glinting tubes, careful to step over the puckered bodies of bats. The red lights flashed on and off and on again.

Tim Gary showed us the low staircase and the oval door the

49

engineers used to enter the turbines for maintenance. He said, "I've been up there. They let me go up. I can see our elm tree, looking out west, and on a clear day, I can count the rooftops."

Mary Lucille asked if there was anything to do about the bats. "There's no good reason they should have to die," she said. "Maybe the turbines can be turned off at night, when bats are liable to go flying."

"That makes no sense," Lawnmower Jill said.

"Yeah. We need all that nighttime wind," Pete said.

"It's not just bats, either. I've seen crows, a couple of hawks," Tim Gary said, "once an eagle."

Mary Lucille clucked her tongue. "The poor things."

"What are you gonna do," Lawnmower Jill said, a skewed smile on her face, "pray for them?"

Mary Lucille's face sank. Abbess Paracleta turned and said, "Lawnmower Jill, that's no way to talk."

Lawnmower Jill said, "It was just a joke."

"Well, it's not funny. It's mean. You're better than that."

It was quiet a while. I wished Frances or Therese or Mary Lucille would come up with something bright to say and change the subject, but the three of them were staring at the grass.

Then, Tim Gary: "You know, another time, I saw a griffin."

"Griffins aren't real," the abbess said. "They're made up."

Tim Gary shrugged. "No, I'm pretty sure it was a griffin."

The abbess shook her head. "Maybe it was a falcon." She sighed. "Probably it was a falcon."

Back at Little Neon, the abbess walked us to the door but stayed on the porch. She said it was time for her to get back to the convent in Providence. She was to lead the rosary at dawn. Tomorrow she would be back to her own work: visiting sick kids in the hospital and overseeing her order's mustard production, marketing, and distribution. (She left a jar of Divine Dijon in the Little Neon fridge. They also made Hallelujah Hot Honey Mustard, she told us, and were looking to get into ketchups and aiolis.) She would come visit soon, she said. She shook our hands, and then she turned to go.

"Wait," Tim Gary said, reaching out his arms. "A hug."

She took hold of Tim Gary and drew him to her and, just as quickly, loosed her arms and was out the door. As she went, I watched her handbag swing.

14.

On a map, the city of Woonsocket looks like a gallbladder. A little pouch. Roads curved and cut at angles that made no sense; they stopped and started and went by new names. You could walk a hundred different stutter streets just to reach the city limits, where the streetlights fell away and the houses were closer to ruin and mutts that looked to be all muscle would bark until you were clear around the next corner. But there wasn't much reason to go to the city limits. Most everything that happened in Woonsocket happened near the river, which ran jagged and cut the city in half. Just north of one of the river's crooks was the library and Ick's Tavern and the Tedeschi, and directly south was Hamlet Street, where the church and the parish and Little Neon sat on the same block as the Catholic high school.

The parish we were to serve was named after Saint Gertrude, the patron saint of cats.

One morning not long after we first arrived, three men came by: the parish priest, the deacon, and the high school principal. I heard Baby answer the door. "Uh-oh," he said. "Who's in trouble?"

Baby made himself scarce once the four of us went to the foyer and ushered the men inside. The principal, Mr. Ruby, looked fifty, with a low ponytail and one slow eye, one quick. Father Steve was maybe thirty, with round wire glasses, his face bright, his voice gentle. Deacon Greg was big-bellied and very old, long wiry hairs poking out of his nostrils. He had a booming voice, as if he was always ready for his turn at the lectern.

Frances offered the men coffee or tea or water or Gatorade or Pepsi or skim milk. Tea, they said, so Therese boiled water and sank tea bags in mugs. It was too hot for tea, but it was too hot for everything.

Mary Lucille yelped when she reached for her mug, and it slipped and crashed to the linoleum. Hot water shot up, and bits of porcelain scattered around the kitchen. Therese groaned. Mary Lucille was always careening into things, getting fingers stuck in doors, dropping whatever she was handed, and Therese was always exasperated.

"Oh, I'm sorry," Mary Lucille said. "I'msorryI'msorry I'msorry."

The four of us stood there and stared at the mess, but the men jumped into action. Father Steve went off and came back with a broom and dustpan and ordered all of us to stay perfectly still. He crouched down with the dustpan, and Deacon Greg used a brush to sweep the white shards up off the floor, and Principal Ruby wiped up the hot water. They were all three very quiet, focused. They kept finding more and more pieces of cup; each time I thought this was the last of it, that surely they had swept it all, one of them pointed across the room, and his eyes lit up, and he said, almost excited, "There. Right there." And they went together to go get it.

When everyone was at the table, Father Steve said how happy the church was to welcome all of us to Woonsocket. He praised Abbess Paracleta's work: she'd created a safe haven for people who needed a place to go.

"See, goodness is somewhere inside these people—these

addicts and felons," Deacon Greg said. "It's somewhere deep down. Lost under all the wreckage." It made me sad, the word "wreckage." As if they were totaled cars. "Your job is to coax the goodness out. By caring for them. Praying with them, giving them hope and faith."

"Yes," Frances said, eyes bright. "I want to extract that goodness."

"Sounds painful, when you put it like that," Mary Lucille said. "Like a tooth."

"I want to make God cool again," Father Steve said. I didn't think God had any interest in being cool, but this I did not say. Father Steve thought we ought to organize a Bible study group. "But a fun one," he said. "Here at Little Neon. Bring in members of the community, help the Neon residents network, socialize, get to know people." He seemed anxious that we agree.

We'd never tried to make the Bible fun. Fun!

Frances said, "Okay," and the rest of us nodded.

"There'll be ups and downs, here at Little Neon," Deacon Greg said. "One day you'll feel like a failure, the next you'll feel like a million bucks. I bet that's not so different from your work in Lackawanna. With the babies."

There was a pause. "Mostly we just felt tired," Therese said.

"I bet," Father Steve said.

The men exchanged a look.

"Well," the principal said. "You came just in time for the loveliest part of the year here in Woonsocket. The summer is glorious. But even as we're enjoying it, we—the father and the deacon and I—we're looking ahead to autumn, and it seems we're in a bit of a jam."

We waited.

"A job's opened up at the high school," he said. "Teaching math. Sophomore geometry. One of our teachers quit on the

54

last day of school. He decided to move to Canada, totally out of the blue. And now we have to find someone to take over his class." He took a sip of tea. "So we were thinking—wow, huh, here we have these bright sisters, new to town, full of energy, lots of enthusiasm, eager to help out, and they love young people—maybe—"

"Maybe one of you could do it," Father Steve said. He looked at each of us.

We were quiet for a moment. Then Mary Lucille said, "Sure."

Therese said, "You're terrible at math, Mary Lucille."

"I wasn't saying I would do it."

"You can take some time to think it over, talk to each other," Deacon Greg said. "You don't have to answer now."

The principal said, "But. We'd appreciate if you could let us know soon, since—"

"What about Agatha?" Frances said, and everyone looked at me. My face flamed. I wanted to vanish.

"What about me?" I said. I hadn't said anything in a while, and my voice came as a whisper.

"Nah," Therese said. "No way. Agatha's too quiet. Those kids will eat her alive."

"She's the smartest of us, though," Mary Lucille said.

"Yeah," Frances said. "I mean, I can't do it. It's clear I'm needed here at Little Neon. And Therese is too impatient. And Mary Lucille's bad at math, like she said. But Agatha—you're bright and kind and remember when you drew the plans for that bird feeder? You have an eye for shapes and things."

I looked at my lap. For years, I'd asked God for faith in myself; my whole life, I'd prayed for a way with words. I'd always wanted to become the kind of person who said the right things, whom other people looked to for answers.

"Like we said, you can take some time to decide, if you

need it," the principal said. "But we'd love to have you." Maybe it wouldn't be so bad, I thought. Maybe it would give me a new way to feel useful.

Mary Lucille touched my arm. She said, "You'd be a great teacher." And despite myself, I smiled.

My smile must have looked like acquiescence, because Frances said, "So it's decided, then. Yeah?"

Deacon Greg asked if we'd like to see the parish, the church, and the gift shop. I followed the black veils of my sisters. On the sidewalk, the sun was hot and high, shining off the deacon's bald spot. The humidity was so thick we could have grabbed at it and held on. We had to blink to adjust to the dim light inside the church. The walls of St. Gertrude's were simple and modern, the high ceiling planked with pine. No scenes of heaven above us. The pews arced around the altar, like seats at an arena.

The men made a great show of demonstrating how to dim the altar lights, how to open the windows, how to slip the holy-water font from the wall so it could be cleaned and refilled. We took turns in front of the alarm system panel, practicing the way to activate and deactivate, and I got it on the first try. To no one in particular, Mary Lucille said, "See, I told you Agatha was the smartest."

15.

I started seeing shades of Little Neon green everywhere I went. Construction workers' vests, the Granny Smiths stacked up in the produce aisle, a pair of tennis balls stuck on the back legs of an old man's walker. On the sidewalk, a boy's sneakers lit up and glowed Little Neon green with each step.

There were other homes like ours in Woonsocket—halfway houses and sober homes—but they were brick, or painted shades of beige. We'd driven past them. They had nothing to do with the church; they were funded by federal agencies and state programs. One was a triple-decker with a porch for sitting. Another was a low bungalow with windows broad enough you could open them and drive a car straight through. They were all so big and sturdy-looking, these houses. They had neat lawns and square hedges, and asters and crocuses in their gardens, and their roofs weren't missing any shingles, and they could house ten times the number of people we could.

"They must have so much room," Therese said once, when we were driving past the three-story house.

"But it's not bright green," Frances said. "It'll never be bright green."

Mary Lucille got it in her head that what everyone in Little Neon needed was a creative outlet. "Watercolors," she said, "or drawing, maybe. A way for people to express themselves visually." Therese thought basketball, but she took a house poll and the results were overwhelmingly in Mary Lucille's favor.

Each Friday, she said, we'd have scheduled art activities, to help people try to "get in touch with the artist within." She acquired a bunch of pencils and scrap paper: we would start with figure drawing. It was obligatory, she said, unless you had to work. And no one had to work.

The first week, she asked Therese to model. "You can wear your clothes. You don't have to be naked," Mary Lucille said.

Therese said, "Duh." She hoisted herself onto the kitchen counter and came to standing, her head an inch from the ceiling. She turned her back to us, a hand on one hip, then swiveled her head around to look past us, a vacant look in her eyes.

Everyone tried to replicate what it was they saw in front of them. I didn't know how it happened, how you could look at something real and make the shape of it show up in pencil. The image was so much more beautiful in my mind than it was on the paper. Something got messed up in the translation. I made her arms look like corn chips.

None of us was very good, except Baby. Baby had sketched Therese's likeness with care: the ratio of her long limbs to the rest of her, the pinched look of her face. He'd made her look human, 3-D. Baby's drawing was good; everybody thought so.

He didn't want to hear it. He didn't like the idea of being called good. "It's not," he said. "Shut up." But I also saw him smile.

16.

The principal brought me a textbook, along with the former teacher's lesson plans, handouts, quizzes, projector slides of Cartesian planes.

Every shape, every theorem looked foreign, to the point that I convinced myself this was some fancy modern geometry, and whatever I'd learned as a teenager had been made obsolete by now. When I thought back to high school geometry, I pictured my white-haired teacher and his blunt mustache. He was peculiar and mean. If you did well on a test, he'd say, "You're on the plane." If you did really well: "You're in first class." If you failed: "You missed the plane. The plane took off and you weren't on board; you didn't make it through security," or, "You don't even have a ticket." He'd say it right there, in front of everyone.

I tried to remember whatever it was the man had said about geometry, but I remembered only his candor, and his mustache, and that the textbook was many inches thick. I hated to carry it to class. I was going through a phase then, always moody and thin-skinned, given to pit stains and crying jags. I assigned significance to the smallest things: my handwriting, the way my sandwich was sliced. But I must not have assigned much significance to geometry, because I couldn't remember a single page of that textbook, except for one sentence: "All squares are rectangles, but not all rectangles are squares."

17.

The heat that summer was brutal. We asked Abbess Paracleta for a window air-conditioning unit, and she told us she did not believe in air-conditioning. She believed in box fans propped in open windows. She believed in Popsicles, cold showers, cross breezes, ice packs on the neck. She believed in getting through it.

Therese told Baby he was lucky: he got to spend his days in the freezer at the ice factory, doing inventory and quality control, and shrink-wrapping whole blocks of ice, while the rest of us were cooked alive. He said it wasn't so great, but it did make him glad for hot evenings. Each week he brought home whole pallets of defective ice for the freezer.

"Defective?" Mary Lucille said.

"There's nothing nasty about it," he said. "It's just some parts turned yellow."

In the attic the air was thick as buttercream. We tried not to complain. Panting one Tuesday night, Frances—red-faced and damp around the collar—went downstairs for a glass of water and came back with a broad bowl of ice. In the kitchen, Baby had suggested she prop it in front of the fan. When she did, we got a cool breeze, enough to help us fall asleep. At dawn we found that the melted ice had been dumped and replaced in the night. "I didn't do anything," Baby said, when we asked.

Days when they didn't have to work, the Neons liked to sit in lawn chairs in the backyard and let the sprinkler strike their legs. I would look out the window and see them sitting side by side. The sprinkler was the kind that whirled around, and the water wasn't sprinkled so much as shot. It came in harsh, violent bursts and made mud of the lawn. But if the water hurt when it hit their shins, the Neons didn't seem to mind. Most afternoons, they fell asleep in their chairs while the sprinkler chopped on. They'd come in hours later, one at a time or all at once, pink from the sun, their shorts clinging to their legs, and drip water throughout the house.

Lawnmower Jill cut the grass every other Saturday, coasting up and down the length of the lawn in her Bronco. On those days, no one was allowed to sit in the yard so long as her engine was running. She was fastidious about cutting precise stripes of grass, and I liked to watch from inside as she charged into the horizon, bits of grass flitting in the air like confetti.

In Woonsocket, Mary Lucille claimed she knew how to cook. She announced this early on, with confidence. She said she was a better cook than any of us. She said she'd learned from watching Mother Roberta. Mother Roberta would make meatballs the size of mangoes. Chicken cacciatore. Pot roast so tender that my mouth waters even now, thinking of it.

Mary Lucille told us she would take on all the cooking in Little Neon.

"Cooking dinner for nine adults, night after night," Therese said. "Are you sure? We can take turns."

"Yes," Mary Lucille said, "I'm sure."

Hot summer evenings, she prepared food that didn't need to be baked or boiled or fried. Fruit salad. Tuna salad sandwiches. Strange things, too: Mashed beans on bread. Sliced turkey on spinach. For Tim Gary, she made yogurt smoothies in various

61

shades of brown. "I wish I got the liquid option," Horse said one night, when Mary Lucille served us walnut tacos: chopped walnuts on tortillas, topped with raw onions and iceberg lettuce and shredded cheese. "Who ever heard of a walnut taco."

Mary Lucille said nothing. We held hands and prayed, and I watched Mary Lucille bring her tortilla mess to her mouth and take a bite. She made a show of chewing and swallowing and saying, "Oh wow, that turned out good." But I saw in her face that she was faking it.

I pretended everything was its own dish: a five-course meal. The raw onion course was awful, but I got it over with first. Last was cheese, the dessert, and after the cheese, I sat for some time without speaking, not because I had nothing to say, but because I was overcome with the sense that our work in Woonsocket would be more difficult than I had imagined. I don't know why it should have been the walnut tacos that revealed this to me, but I guess it was as good a moment as any.

We'd come to Woonsocket to care for these people, but we had no idea what that meant. We thought we had things to give them, prayer and compassion and mercy and home-cooked meals, but none of this seemed like enough.

It's truer to say that we—or, I, at least—had come because we'd been told it was God's plan, which a lot of the time has nothing to do with what you had in mind for yourself.

18.

It wasn't long after the walnut tacos that I found a pair of stiff-heeled roller skates in the garage. They were brown leather, and a size too small for me, but I tried them on anyhow. Tight in the toe, but they laced up fine.

I had this recurring image in my head of Mother Roberta at the grocery store, pushing a cart and lifting her feet so she took off down the aisle, the chrome of the cart gleaming under the lights. "Yeehaw!" she yelled, making us all laugh. It wasn't the same thing, I knew, but still I was excited about the skates in a way that felt illicit. I hadn't roller-skated since a grade school birthday. I hadn't done something for the fun of it in maybe forever.

I waited until after evening prayer, when everyone else was in bed, and then I snuck to the garage in my nightgown.

I never told the others. It was the first decision I made on my own in Woonsocket, the first thing I kept to myself. No permission, no approval, no company. No one to sidetrack me from what I wanted, which was to soar across the cement. It would be easy, I thought, like walking, but more fun.

Well: it was hard to lift one foot and then the other. There I was, graceless and inept, doubled over but determined. For stability I groped the walls, but I still fell down hard. Blood bloomed on my hands and knees, and sweat collected around my collar and pits, but I kept on, up and up and up again, from one end of the garage to the other, until my mouth was dry with the work of it. When I heard footsteps, I froze, and when there were no more footsteps I took myself across the cement again.

After a while, when I was too tuckered out to try again, I went inside and drank cold water and iced my knees in the kitchen.

Tim Gary came down from his room to find me pressing Baby's defective ice cubes to my knees, the skates abandoned on the linoleum.

"Hi," he said. He gestured at the skates. "Where'd you find those?"

I reddened. I said, "The garage."

"You skinned your knees."

"Yeah," I said. The ice cubes were melting down my shins. "I'm sorry—I hope I didn't wake you?"

He shook his head. "I was awake. Came down for a glass of milk."

I told him to sit. I could pour him milk. I chucked what was left of the ice cubes in the sink. In search of a tall glass, I dripped pink water all over the kitchen floor, opening and closing every cupboard door. Little Neon's kitchen was still foreign to me. I picked all the wrong cupboards.

When the milk was poured, I turned to Tim Gary. Where could I find a straw?

He had just the one straw, he said, the one he had used at dinner, and he drank from it at every meal. His ex-wife had brought it with a milkshake after his jaw operation. A time, I could see, when her patience was broader and her love less finite.

I looked in the trash and found the straw; one of us had tossed it. It was still in good shape, not crushed or kinked. I rinsed it in hot water and slipped it into the thick white milk, and I watched Tim Gary drink, his soft throat rippling as the milk disappeared.

He looked up and said, "I can teach you to skate." He used to be a hockey player, he said. Roller skates were no big deal. He was sure it wouldn't take me long to get the hang of it.

I said, as a reflex, "Oh, that's so nice, thank you, but I can learn on my own, really; I'm so bad; you don't have to; don't worry."

And he said, "Why would I be worried?"

We met in the garage the next night, after curfew, after dark. I made him promise not to tell anyone. My sisters were in bed; we'd said our nightly rosary. Lawnmower Jill, Baby, Pete, and Horse were in the front room playing gin rummy, but no one seemed to notice us slip out the kitchen door.

"I stole Pete's construction gear," Tim Gary said, and knelt to strap pads to my knees. He was all business. "So you don't get all beat up." I lifted the hem of my nightgown an inch so he could bring the Velcro around. "Okay," he said, when he was done. "Show me what you got."

I launched myself from where I was standing, and a second later I was flat on the ground.

"Okay. We'll start with little steps," he said. His voice was firm, no-nonsense. "Stand up and walk with your heels together, toes pointed out." He watched me do it. "Now, add a little glide," he said. "Push off with one foot, glide with the other." I tried. "Now, squat. Get a little closer to the ground. Not that low. Okay. Right, push off and glide, push off and glide, push off and—whoops! Okay, get back up."

For a second I stayed on the ground, belly-up, laughing and

moaning at the same time. I'd skinned an elbow, and blood came through a fresh hole in my nightgown sleeve. Tim Gary gave me a hand back up.

When I got the push-and-glide part down, Tim Gary taught me how to stop: you drag a toe. Then he told me about turning: you cross the opposite leg up and over, and you push and lean and glide where you want to go.

I was sweating, smiling, ready to practice as many turns as I could make in the two-car garage. But then Tim Gary pulled the garage door up and said next I had to make my way to the end of the driveway and back.

I looked out past the hood of the white van: beyond it was nothing but night.

"Come on," he said. "Be the first Neon to break curfew."

"No way," I said. "I'll fall and die. Or the abbess will kill me."

"No one has to find out."

I'm still not sure what scared me more as I stood and looked into the dark with little wheels on my feet: staying there, or not staying there. But the night looked lovely and wild and immense, and so I lunged headlong onto the driveway before I could talk myself out of it. The only sound was the skate wheels spinning on the blacktop and thwacking over the cracks and then I was there, on the street, and I dragged my right toe to stop. When I turned around Little Neon looked blue in the night, and I could see that Tim Gary was grinning, radiant under the bare bulb that hung in the garage. He called to me in a whisper that was also a shout. "You did it! You did it!"

Later, upstairs, the others were snoring at different speeds. No one roused when I lifted my sheets and slipped into bed.

19.

Pete liked to mail a page of the newspaper or a Xeroxed poem to his friend Manny, whom he'd met in Central Falls, in prison.

Manny still had three years left of his sentence and didn't have anyone on the outside but Pete. Days off from the granite yard, Pete took the bus to visit Manny, or he'd go to the greyhound track and watch dogs race, and, twice a month, he got a ride to a facility in Cranston, where he'd sit with his nine-year-old daughter and color with Magic Markers while a supervisor watched. To Cranston he wore a shirt that buttoned and pants he'd ironed, and each week he came downstairs with all three of his neckties and asked which we thought he ought to wear. One Sunday, he allotted extra time so he could bring his daughter a Happy Meal, but by the time he arrived, the fries were cold and limp.

Prison's where Pete started reading poetry. In Little Neon he always had a book of poems with him, and he was fastidious about returning them to the library on time and always came home with another. He recited whole stanzas from memory, often without provocation. He was in a big Anne Sexton phase. I think I liked the recitations more than the others did. "Thank you," Therese said, every time he finished a poem, but it sounded as if she was only glad he'd reached the end.

Pete sent Manny some Sexton or a page from the sports section or sometimes world news. I asked Pete if it wouldn't be better to send a whole section of the newspaper, so Manny could finish articles that were spread out over multiple pages, but he said he didn't have the stamps for that.

I told Father Steve we needed money for stamps. Before we'd left Lackawanna, Mother Roberta had advised us to write to the new pope—introduce ourselves, tell him we'd be praying for him, and ask that he pray for us in our new vocation in Rhode Island.

"Sending mail to the Vatican is expensive," I told Father Steve.

He let us buy five hundred-stamp rolls. When I showed Pete, he said, "Now Manny will know how everything ends."

One morning I looked through the paper before Pete had woken up. There was an article in the metro section about church leaders in California, who'd written many checks of many thousands to keep many people quiet. I pulled the page from the paper and tore it into shreds over the trash can. I told myself I was protecting Pete, and Manny, too, but really I was protecting the church.

When we first heard rumors like these, Mother Roberta told us to listen, and to read the Bible, and to pray. We listened, and we read the Bible, and we prayed. When there were new articles with new names, we prayed some more. No matter how much we prayed, there were always new names. I asked Mother Roberta if we were praying hard enough. "I'm sure you are," she said. "Don't give up."

20.

We spent half an hour writing letters to the pope on sheets of paper torn from a yellow legal pad. It seemed to me we should use better paper with a bit of weight, or at least paper that wasn't yellow. But Frances said, with undue authority, "The pope doesn't care what kind of paper we use."

I didn't see why it was so easy for everyone else to come up with things to write. They were flying, as if it were an exam and they had prepared in advance and were now afraid of running out of time. They grabbed and filled second and third sheets of paper while I was still trying to finish my first. And then I felt even worse when it was decided we ought to read ours aloud to each other. It was as if I'd responded to the wrong prompt. I'd written about the things that I hoped the pope would address, and the others had written the stories of their lives.

Therese told the pope how she'd been in awe of the nuns she'd known growing up, especially her high school track coach, Sister Geraldine, who taught her to pray before and after the starting gun, keep her knees up and her hands loose. Therese ran faster and longer when she asked for God's intervention. She won medals and championships, and college coaches called her at her parents' house to promise her glory, scholarships, free sneakers, all the yellow Gatorade she could drink. But when it came time to take the SAT, Therese skipped the test and donated the fifteen-dollar testing fee to the convent. Sister Geraldine told her God had great things in store for her.

Mary Lucille's letter read like a confession. She detailed how she'd left an old boyfriend to pursue religious life. For the pope, she avoided going into detail about this phase of her life, but we all remembered how she used to talk of Hank. She had lived with him, she told us, and she claimed they'd loved each other, but there was a pink crater on her neck where Hank had put out a cigarette, and a bald section of her scalp where she'd pulled out all her hair in those first months, when he would call the convent every day and ask to speak to her. Early on, she used to talk to us about how much she missed Hank, and some nights when we were novices I could hear her weep in the dark, but the closer we got to taking our vows, the less she mentioned him, and we were careful to never ask. She told the pope that she'd been blind, all those years; God was the real love of her life all along.

Frances wrote about how she'd known since she was a girl that she owed her life to God. As a girl she was a Bible fanatic; she could not get enough. She went on every mission trip, silent retreat, and pilgrimage she could find. She daydreamed of parables and built dioramas displaying the lives of the saints. Her mother was horrified when she decided to become a sister, but it was only because she didn't understand. The moments Frances felt most useful and alive, she told the pope, had always been the moments she spent with her hands folded in prayer.

And I? I asked the pope to consider the poor. I told him, in not so vexed a tone, that he needed to choose whom he'd serve: the people, or the priests. After the others were reading what they'd written, I told them I hadn't finished mine yet; it wasn't ready.

"Oh, come on," Therese said. "Who cares. Just read what you have."

I shook my head.

"Agatha," Frances said. "We all read our letters. It's only fair."

Mary Lucille said, "She doesn't have to read it if she doesn't want to. You're not the boss." But then Therese lunged across the table and tried to pry the letter from my hands. My face hot, I pulled it free and tore it into pieces while she watched.

"What's the big deal?" Therese said, and when I didn't say anything, she crossed her arms. "Well. I guess you'll have to start over, then."

I did eventually write a new letter, but I still didn't write about myself. I wrote about pews. I told the pope that I noticed very few people sit up close to the altar. Most churchgoers liked to stay near the back, near the exit, as if they wanted to keep a safe distance from the pulpit, or they thought they'd need a quick escape to the world outside. But the exception was my sisters and me. We always sat in the first pew. We always got as close as we were told we could.

21.

Mary Lucille and I sat near the kitchen window and watched Therese on the driveway. It was the middle of the afternoon, and she was up on a ladder, taking a scissors to the old rope net on the basketball hoop. I could hear her muttering to herself each time she worked the scissors: "Take that! And that!" When it was free, she chucked it to the ground.

She was sweating through her habit, stopping every few minutes to mop her brow. She'd just lifted the new net to thread the loops onto the rim when Tim Gary came into the kitchen. He looked through a drawer a moment, then said, "Have you seen the scissors?" He wanted to cut his hair.

Mary Lucille said Therese had them outside. She said, "You should let Agatha do it. She cuts all our hair."

It was true: twice a year, whenever we changed the clocks, I lopped inches from my sisters' hair. I was limited in my technique—Therese got a blond bob, Frances a shorter brown bob. Mary Lucille wore her hair cropped close, with a curtain-like look. Her hair was thick and the color of dust. The three of them trusted me. I felt close to them those afternoons, memorizing their cowlicks and ears.

I told Tim Gary I'd be glad to, and he said okay. "I do have a hard time reaching the back."

He wet his hair under the kitchen sink and dragged a folding chair to the backyard. Therese was finished with the scissors, which were enormous, more like hedge trimmers than hair-cutting shears. I stood behind him and took some hair in my fingers. Up close, I could see the scars on his face: they looked like puckered seams.

Therese was practicing layups, flouncing in her habit, and Mary Lucille sat near the blacktop and gave her feedback. After she sank a shot, Mary Lucille said, "Bingo!"

Tim Gary closed his eyes. "I like it short on the sides," he said. "And I part it on the left."

"You got it," I said.

After a minute, he said, "I used to think if I grew my hair long maybe it would create an optical illusion, and make it look like I still had a whole jaw. But it just looked like I needed a haircut."

I trimmed around his ears, and Therese missed a shot. "That's okay, that's okay," Mary Lucille said. "Next time."

"You're distracting me," Therese said.

"Okay, I'll be quiet."

Therese sank the next shot.

"Hot diggity dog!" Mary Lucille cried, and Therese shot her a look. "Sorry. Sorry."

I took a half inch off on the sides of Tim Gary's head, then lifted the hair on top and closed the scissors along the edges of my fingers. When I finished cutting, I blew the bits of hair from his shoulders, and Tim Gary turned to look at himself in the kitchen window. "Hot diggity dog," he said, "to borrow a phrase. It's perfect. Thank you." I smiled big. "Come on, Mary Lucille," he said, waving her over. "Let's see about fixing a bird feeder to this tree."

I felt my heart bulge. The other Neons avoided us sisters, like dogs dodging a vacuum. They exhibited little interest in getting to know us or letting us get to know them. Even Pete had little to say to me that wasn't about stamps. They always had other places to be, other people to talk to. But Tim Gary was the exception. He didn't mind finding himself in our company. He liked to have us around.

22.

Frances went to work designing promotional materials for the Bible study. She'd thought she'd stay busy gardening vegetables, but she planted one packet of radicchio seeds and then got bored. "Forget vegetables," she said. "These people don't need vegetables. What they need is sacred texts."

The meetings would start in September, once a week every Tuesday at 7:00 p.m., but she wanted to start spreading the word. She had Father Steve make an announcement at the end of each Mass. She put an ad in the missive. On the parish computer she designed a flyer. She'd used a free template, and it came with a picture of a spotted dog in the middle.

"Why is there a dog?" Therese asked, looking at a copy in the kitchen. I was at the table, reading the geometry textbook.

"I couldn't figure out how to get rid of it," Frances said. "The template was a flyer for a lost pet."

"It's cute," Mary Lucille said. "Let's keep it."

"But a dog has nothing to do with the Bible," Therese said.

"Maybe I can include a disclaimer that there's not actually a dog involved," Frances said, but then Therese told her it wasn't hard to delete the dog. The next flyer Frances printed out had no dog, but to make up for the space, she'd made the word STUDY larger than all the other words. And she'd included a picture of a Communion wafer next to a glass of Eucharistic wine.

"It looks a little scary," Therese said. "Like we're yelling. And why is there wine? People will think we'll be serving booze."

Frances told Therese if she was so smart, she could design

the flyer herself, and Therese came back with something taste-ful and simple, with tear-off information slips on the bottom. "It's perfect," Mary Lucille said, and Frances looked but didn't say a word.

It was a relief not to have to talk to anyone about my work. We'd had a conversation about all this: the three of them would take over organizing the Bible study while I taught math. "You can still come, of course," Frances said. "You just don't have to do anything."

They discussed their plans for Bible study all the time. They wanted to welcome anyone, from any religious background, as long as they were at least fifteen. Their plan was to start from Genesis and go all the way to the very last book, Revelation.

"How long will that take?" I asked.

They looked at each other. Frances shrugged and said, "As long as it takes."

There was more reading involved in geometry than I remem-bered. Each theorem was a long, complex sentence, and you had to know what all the words meant in order to try to un-derstand it.

After morning prayer, I studied at the kitchen table. I stud-ied while I waited for my turn in the shower. I studied when I was supposed to be asleep. I solved every problem in the back of the book, found the area of each circle and trapezoid. I learned words for the way the world was built: "perpendicular" and "parallel" and "congruent."

But it didn't feel like enough. To know something is one kind of work, and to turn it into speech is another kind en-tirely. I was good at memorization. But how would I say it all out loud?

I became so overcome with anxiety that one night I took Mary Lucille aside in the attic. She was the one whose compassion was most easily tapped.

"You already know more than they do," Mary Lucille told me, though I could tell she, too, only half believed it.

It took all my courage to articulate how I was feeling. "I'm afraid," I said.

"Aw, Agatha," she cooed, and cocked her head. "Just do what Mother Roberta would do. Don't speak until you know the right words."

In the dark, I stared at the ceiling and wondered what it felt like, to know the right words.

23.

It was the rule: in order to get a free donut, you had to go to church. You couldn't wait at home until Mass ended and duck into donut time, or ask someone to bring you one. There were no shortcuts.

Pete and Tim Gary had no trouble finding something of value in Mass; Pete, in particular, was a sucker for psalms. But Baby, Horse, and Lawnmower Jill couldn't stand Mass. For them, it was drudgery. It was cruel and unusual punishment. Baby thought it wasn't worth the donut, and Horse and Lawnmower Jill agreed, but the church had air-conditioning, and that was enough to draw them from their beds in the summer.

One Sunday in late July, Mary Lucille volunteered to work the crying room, and Lawnmower Jill decided to go with her. She thought it'd be less boring than sitting in the nave. She was wearing her purple parka and cutoff jean shorts.

"Won't you be hot?" Therese said.

"No," Lawnmower Jill said. "I use it like a purse." By way of demonstration, she slipped a banana into a pocket.

"You might have to change a diaper," Mary Lucille warned her. "Or clean spit-up. Or calm a baby down. Or have your hair yanked. You have to be ready for anything. You never know what's going to happen in the crying room."

Lawnmower Jill said, "Bring it on."

It is a pleasant thing, to be read to, even when you aren't really listening. Father Steve's homily was about many things:

adolescence, Iran-Contra, a man who purchased thousands of dollars' worth of Healthy Choice pudding, taxes, white flight, something called a skipjack, and Adam and Eve. The AC was cranked high, and huge industrial fans were blasting so loud, his voice got lost on its way from the pulpit.

Horse was nodding off. I gave her a nudge, and she blinked and sat upright. Father Steve liked to strum a guitar while he sang hymns—he hated the organ, called it "stodgy," felt it had no place in modern worship—and each song was like a lullaby.

Pete was the first to find a feather: one floated down and landed on his knee. Another appeared, and they kept coming one by one, then all at once. At the altar, Father Steve was busy transubstantiating, too lost in the task to notice until everyone in the pews was already smiling about it: the church had filled with fine white feathers. The fans sent them high, like snow in reverse. We watched the tiniest of them drift down, and just when we reached and tried to grab them, they'd catch the breeze and rise back up. They hovered and spun mid-flight, turned up and over themselves, drifted and dipped in faltering arcs.

Someone sneezed, then sneezed again.

"Oh, wow," Father Steve said into the microphone, when he looked out from the pulpit, chalice in his hand. The whole spectacle was marvelous, and absurd; I was helpless with wonder.

Horse said, "Oh my God, look."

We turned to see what she was pointing at: Lawnmower Jill was standing in the back of the church, beaming. She held a baby in one arm, and she'd split the sleeve of her coat open so the baby could reach into the nylon and pull out the down inside and toss handfuls of feathers into the air. She kept tearing open new sections of her coat and giving the baby more feathers to send into the air. The baby was giggling, flinging her head back so she could see all the tiny bits of plumage levitate. I smiled to see it.

"What in the Sam Hill," Frances whispered.

"She's acting like a child," Therese said, and she stepped over everyone's feet on her way out of the pew. She started down the aisle, feathers clinging to her as she went. The baby's mother got there first and held out her hands for Lawnmower Jill to give her the baby. When she didn't, the woman yanked the baby from Lawnmower Jill's hands. Then Therese took Lawnmower Jill by the elbow and led her up the aisle to sit in our pew.

"Okay, people," Father Steve said. "Kill the fans."

Someone switched them off, and the feathers dropped slowly onto our heads. We lined up for Communion in a daze. I knew, waiting in line, that I was supposed to be solemnly reflecting on the significance of the Eucharist, but I was still giddy with delight, busy picking feathers from the folds of my habit when Father Steve held a wafer in front of my face and said, "Body of Christ." I needed a second to remember to say, "Amen."

24.

It took Lawnmower Jill nearly six hours to sweep up all the feathers and vacuum out all the air-conditioning vents. Deacon Greg had her clean out all the holy-water fonts, too, where the feathers had clotted together.

We decided not to tell Abbess Paracleta about the feathers, but Frances still felt it was important to come up with a way to punish Lawnmower Jill. In the garage she pulled out Lawnmower Jill's file so she could make a note of her "misconduct," as she called it. In the folder Frances learned that Lawnmower Jill had lived in Rhode Island all her life. She'd been raised by other people's parents: in foster homes, a group home, and, for eighteen months when she was sixteen, a juvenile detention center. She got a flu shot every year. She had once stabbed the dog of a sworn enemy. Another time she drove her car into the public pool after a near-fatal number of Narragansetts. She did not believe in God. But she could, the abbess noted, be convinced to pray.

When we worked in the day care, we'd read books about disciplining young children, and we'd all come away with different ideas as to what was best. Therese believed in withholding. She wanted to refuse Lawnmower Jill dinner.

I didn't see what the big deal was. "She already cleaned it all up," I said. "Besides, she's a grown woman."

"Maybe the answer is positive reinforcement," Mary Lucille said.

"Oh, so we should shower her with praise every time she decides not to make a giant mess?" Therese said.

"I didn't say that," Mary Lucille said.

"Let's just talk to her," Frances said.

So when Lawnmower Jill came home from work, Frances asked her if she might take a little walk with us, and she said she was tired, and Frances said she didn't really have a choice, and Mary Lucille said please, and then Lawnmower Jill said fine. Therese and Frances walked up front, next to her, and Mary Lucille and I walked behind them.

She knew what was coming. "I was just taking the baby for a walk," Lawnmower Jill said, before anyone could say anything. "She wouldn't stop fussing, and she liked the sound of the music coming from the church, and then she grabbed at a loose feather, and she was so happy when the fan made it fly—"

"I understand," Mary Lucille said, craning her neck to be heard. "You were just trying to distract her."

"No, I was trying to make her happy," Lawnmower Jill said. "Which is different."

Frances said, "But, well. It got out of control. You can't just give a baby everything she wants. You can't indulge every cry. You have to learn to say no."

Lawnmower Jill stopped walking. "Everything is some kind of moral issue with you people," she said. I felt my pulse race. The four of us looked at her and watched her composure come to pieces. "I'm sick of it. It makes my blood boil. Have you ever noticed that I don't give two shits? Or even one shit? No, no— half a shit. I don't give half a shit what you think. No, in fact, take a shit and cut it into eighths—no, sixteenths, and one of those sixteenths is more precious to me than anything you have to say, about anything, ever."

We stared. After a moment Lawnmower Jill said, "Fuck it," and marched off in the direction home.

When she was out of earshot, Frances crossed her arms and sighed. "This will have to go in her file."

25.

I lay in bed that night and thought of Mother Roberta, how sometimes rage shot through her and turned her electric. There was this memory I kept returning to: one afternoon Father Thaddeus had made her angry, and I saw her push a leather armchair so hard it turned up and over itself.

It was never any one thing that made Mother Roberta angry; it was everything together. I imagined that her personal litany of grievances ran through her mind at all times, like endless ticker tape. Disappointments of every size and scale. Even when she wasn't outwardly angry, there was always a reminder that she had been, once, or was still, silently: the frown lines between her brows; the way she walked heavy, heels first and hulking; the shards of broken glass in the sink.

Now I think it had something to do with love. The church she loved had never become what she wanted; the church she'd loved all her life was reluctant to change. She had no interest in controlling her temper because she had no idea how to control her love.

26.

After dinner one night Tim Gary asked if anyone wanted to walk to the big tire and back. It was a half mile to where a big black monster truck tire had washed up on the riverbank. The methadone made his stomach upset and he could use some air, he said. Therese and I went with him. As we walked, he told us a story about his ex-wife.

The winter Tim Gary fell sick, his wife took him to the Sears in Warwick. It had been forever since he'd been in a mall. They stood together on the same stair of the escalator, and it brought them high up into the air, and in the space between one floor and the next, he and his wife let go of each other's hands and looked out at the wild terrain: noisy and sleek and bright, aglow with colors and humming with life. They soared up over the food court and leaned their heads back: above them was a ceiling so high and vast and luminous, it was as if the sky they'd known—the place from which balloons never returned, blue and dreamy and faraway—had been replaced with this new pale heaven.

His wife, he told us, was smarter and had seen more of the world than he. She read the newspaper and muttered to herself about what was there. She went on long walks to be away from him. The mall was one of their last voyages together, and Tim Gary felt close to her in that moment, this woman who locked herself in the bathroom each morning, who had stopped accompanying him to the hospital to sit next to him during his treatments. He wished in that moment that the escalator ride would never end—that the great big staircase would carry them up above the ceiling, above the troposphere, and his wife and he could grip the handrail and watch the people below them eat pizza, the pretty pepperonis getting smaller and smaller until they were microscopic, until they were so small they could not be seen.

And then something snagged, and he was flat on the floor, staring up at the man-made ceiling. He cried out and struggled to free the bootlace that had caught in the escalator's teeth. He looked up to his wife, and she glanced at him, but she did not kneel to help. She stood above him, arms crossed. She laughed as if she'd seen it coming, as if she'd known all along he wasn't ready for something as sophisticated as the escalator, and chances were he'd never be.

When we reached the tire, Tim Gary asked us if we thought the tire would stay there forever. Each of us tried to move it with our hands and feet, but none of us could make it budge, so we all agreed that it wasn't going anywhere anytime soon.

27.

Mary Lucille came home with a big bag of art supplies from the thrift. Squares of felt, mismatched gel pens, plastic beads in tubes, clumps of nylon yarn, loose sequins, dried-up markers and paints. Every Friday we'd try something new, she said. Every week a new project.

She'd found enough watercolor sets for everyone to share, so we all sat side by side at the kitchen table. "Why do we have to?" said Lawnmower Jill, and Mary Lucille said it was for the enrichment of her soul, to which Lawnmower Jill groaned.

It was dark and warm, quiet except for the whir of the fan in the window. We were hunched over our paints when Abbess Paracleta came through the front door.

"What's all this?" she asked, standing in the kitchen.

"We're painting," Horse said. She held up her paper. "Mine's an alien."

"How fun," the abbess said. "I brought soup." She held up a plastic tub of green liquid.

"Thank you. Join us," Therese said. "Pull up a stool."

The abbess put the soup in the fridge and then came to the table to paint. Mary Lucille gave her a spare brush and a sheet of paper.

"I'm afraid I'm not very good," the abbess said, staring at the bright discs of paint in front of her.

"Neither is anyone at this table," Therese said, "except Baby." His cheeks flamed, but he didn't look up.

Mary Lucille decided to tape everyone's paintings to the wall behind the corduroy couch. The paper was water-warped, the paintings slapdash. But I liked to look at them all together. Lawnmower Jill's had turned into a gradient of brown where unlike colors found each other. Tim Gary had made the exact right shade of green to paint Little Neon: a lot of yellow and a little blue. There was Horse's purple alien, and Lawnmower Jill's black Cadillac, and Baby's red cardinal, and Pete's bananas. And the abbess's dragonfly, Therese's mountain, and Mary Lucille's horse (more of a rhinoceros), and Frances's daisy, and my evergreen tree.

Therese stood on a step stool and poised each painting in the air, and Tim Gary stood back and told her how to move the paper. "Left, left, left, a little more left, okay, lift the right side just a—stop. Yes. Perfect." He did this for each piece of paper, and when they were all stuck on the wall, he looked more pleased than I'd ever seen him.

The abbess stayed for a glass of water, into which she squirted Metamucil from a bottle she kept in her purse. It turned opaque, the color of cantaloupe.

"That soup I brought will heat up beautifully," she said, "for dinner tomorrow."

"What kind?" Horse said.

"Split pea," the abbess said, and Horse made a face. "You're lucky it's not cabbage," the abbess said in response. And then with no prelude, she asked about everyone's sobriety. She was blunt; she had no time for liars. She looked each Neon in the eye and asked them if they'd been using. And when everyone said no, ma'am, she asked us if the pee tests were coming back clean.

It was Therese who was handling everyone's urine Monday mornings. She was the only one who had the stomach for it.

She held each warm cup that was handed to her and called it a "specimen." She had to wait five minutes for the panel on the front to change colors; then she had me confirm everything. The cups tested for meth and pot and pain pills and crack cocaine and ketamine and a whole bunch of things I'd never heard of, and there was a little test strip for each one. "Is that two lines there?" Therese would ask, holding a cup in the air, up to the light, and I would look and say yes. Two lines was good. One line was bad. So far we'd only ever had two lines.

When Therese told the abbess all the specimens were coming back clean, the abbess looked happy. She asked how everyone had been enjoying Mass, and Lawnmower Jill crossed her arms and slumped in her chair. Tim Gary said, "I like it."

"Good man," the abbess said. "Keep it up, and you never know how you might be rewarded. You might just meet someone. Someone special. Any of you might."

"Nah," Tim Gary said. "Doubt it."

"Plenty of people go to church to find love," the abbess said. "It's why I went, when I was younger. I was sixteen. I learned how to put on lipstick, and I wanted boys to see me. Church was the best place to be on display."

On display! I laughed: I'd never imagined vanity on the list of reasons a person might find themself in a pew. I'd assumed Abbess Paracleta was the kind of nun whose faith developed before her gums had teeth.

Mary Lucille always thrilled to a love story. "Did it work?" she asked. "Did boys notice you?"

"Some of them worked up the nerve to ask me out," the abbess said, matter-of-factly, "but I didn't give them the time of day. It was easy to turn them down. I got so taken with God, I didn't have eyes for anyone else."

"That's how it was for me," Frances said, wistful.

"Not me," Tim Gary said. "I wasn't getting asked out in high school, and I wasn't getting close to God, either." Church didn't make him feel good, he said, when he was younger. He didn't develop much of a way with God. "Church was always just digging up the worst parts of me."

"But what about now?" Therese asked.

"Now it feels like it's the only thing that'll keep me going." He stared at his lap. "I'm all out of alternatives; I've tried everything else."

"You know, there's a verse in Deuteronomy," Mary Lucille said. "'Be not afraid, for God goes with you; He will not forsake you.'"

"Or how about Isaiah," Therese said. "'Those who hope in the Lord will soar on eagles' wings.'"

"Griffins' wings, too," Baby said, smiling at Tim Gary.

"They're real, dammit," Tim Gary said, but he smiled back.

Abbess Paracleta had a psalm about how God turns mourning into dancing.

"Sisters," Lawnmower Jill said. "Enough. Please. Enough of the Bible."

But they kept going. They took turns listing verses. They had an endless supply. A lot of the lines they quoted seemed only tenuously related to Tim Gary's situation. But he was patient. He sat still as they recited.

And then, when they'd run out of things to say, he said, "I hope that all turns out to be true. I really do hope."

"'Need is not quite belief,'" Pete said. After a moment: "That's Anne Sexton."

28.

Lawnmower Jill went missing on baked potato night. She didn't come home for dinner, and then she didn't come home for bed.

We stayed by the front window, watching the dark, starting at everyone who walked under the streetlamp. After curfew, when there was no sign of her, Frances called the abbess, and the abbess didn't answer.

We panicked; we were on edge. We decided to split up. Two would stay home and wait, and the other two would walk to the Tedeschi, where Lawnmower Jill worked, and ask after her.

"Agatha and I will go," Therese said. She stepped into her shoes and bent to tie them.

"But I wanted to," Mary Lucille said.

"Stay here and wait," Therese said, without even turning her head.

Therese and I didn't speak a word. We rushed down the street in the dark, our habits swishing. The Tedeschi was so brightly lit we could spot it from blocks away. Up close it was even brighter. When we swung the door open, a bell chimed, and all of the store was spread before us: aisles stacked with candy bars and puffed-up bags of chips, a whole wall of refrigerated beverages standing upright. In the corner, glossy hot dogs turned over themselves on a rack.

The girl behind the register looked about nineteen. She wore a red apron over her pregnant belly and took a swig from a jug of orange pop. The name tag pinned to her apron said "Mickey." "Can I help you?" she said.

We told her we were looking for Lawnmower Jill. It took

Mickey a minute to understand what we wanted her for, since Mickey was right there and could point us to whatever aisle we needed, but when Therese told her Lawnmower Jill didn't come home for dinner, Mickey said, "Oh. Hmm. She'd never miss dinner."

Mickey told us to check the park, or the riverbank near the bridge, or Ick's tavern. We checked the river, and then started toward Ick's, but two blocks in we stopped.

"Her Bronco," Therese said, plaintive, pointing ahead. The mower was parked a half a block up on Getchell Avenue, outside a triple-decker. I recognized it: one of the other halfway houses.

"What do we do?" I said.

"Maybe she's just gone in to visit a friend," Therese said.

When we called the abbess in the morning, she said she already knew. Lawnmower Jill had told her she wanted out. She was tired, she'd said, of people acting as if God was worth her time. Then Getchell had an opening, and she was next on their waitlist. She'd left with all her stuff in a backpack, without goodbye.

You can't make someone stay, the abbess said. You can't force someone to change.

"Why didn't you tell us?" Frances asked the abbess.

"I had to wait for the paperwork to process."

The four of us searched for information on the parish computer the next day. The place was called Getchell House. Women only. They offered a four-phase transition program lasting six months, including daily meetings. No one was asked to pray. Everyone had a private room.

"But it's not bright green," Frances said.

It wasn't the first time we'd been left. In Lackawanna, women left us all the time. They chose lives outside the convent and left in the middle of the night. Every time, it hurt until it didn't.

We were never to speak of the women who gave up religious life, so I don't know if the others prayed for them as often as I did, on my knees before bed every night. I pictured their faces one after another, until, at some point, other worries eclipsed them, and I forgot, when I folded my hands, to list their names.

So we'd been left before. But precedent is no comfort.

At dinner, Mary Lucille mashed the leftover baked potatoes and fried a long flap of flank steak. She gave Tim Gary milk and oatmeal. And when the food was on the table, she said, without fanfare, "Lawnmower Jill has moved out."

She found another place to live, Therese explained, somewhere more in line with what she needed.

Everyone was quiet for a moment. I saw the ways everyone's faces twisted up—some in confusion, others in hurt.

Then Horse said, "Fuck. I knew it."

Pete said, "Which house is she at?"

"We're not at liberty to say," Therese said.

Horse said, "Did she say why she left?"

Mary Lucille shook her head.

"But she's okay," Tim Gary said. "Right?"

"She's okay," Frances said, as much to herself as to them. "She's okay."

We didn't want to talk about it: the sense that we had failed. There wasn't anything good to say, so no one brought it up. But it was heavy in the air between us, in the glances and silences. When the lawn needed mowing, one of us said, "The lawn needs mowing," and we stared at the grass from the kitchen window. Eventually Therese found an iron push mower in the garage, and she spent the better part of a Tuesday afternoon forcing it up the yard and back. She sweated through the back of her habit,

93

her face red with the effort. "At least it makes no noise," she said when she came inside.

Everyone seemed to think we needed more of what we had. More art, said Mary Lucille. More exercise, said Therese. More Bible, said Frances.

In bed I pictured Lawnmower Jill preparing to go: sorting through her things, balling up socks and underwear and corduroys and shoving them deep in her backpack. I wondered if she thought to pack toothpaste. Or a toothbrush. Or soap. But probably her new home gave her the things she needed, and none of the things she didn't want.

More listening, I thought. I thought we should probably listen more.

29.

At night, alone in the back bedroom, Horse couldn't sleep. She'd lie awake for hours, and then if she fell asleep, she'd end up screaming herself awake. She dreamed about electrification and vaginal prolapse and polar bears eating her alive. At breakfast she'd relay every detail of her nightmares, her eyes wide, darting between our faces. She picked at her bottom lip with her fingernails, making it bleed.

We were uneasy. We knew the trouble: Lawnmower Jill was gone. But we didn't know what to tell Horse, or what to do.

We pooled our money and bought a phone card so we could call Mother Roberta long-distance. She would know.

We went to the parish office and sat around a table, and Therese punched the buttons on the speakerphone. We all stared at it. The receptionist picked up on the first ring, but after Therese asked for Mother Roberta, it was a while until she came to the phone.

Mother Roberta would turn eighty-two soon. I tried to imagine her in her new home, but I didn't know how to picture the place. In my head I defaulted to a place exactly like where I'd seen her last, our old convent in Lackawanna, with walls the color of mayonnaise.

When she picked up the receiver, she didn't need to ask who it was. "I was wondering when you'd call," she said. Her voice was like a balm. "I've been thinking of the four of you. You'll never believe what we had for dinner."

Mary Lucille said, "Lasagna."

"It wasn't lasagna." There was a pause, then: "Pancakes! We had pancakes—for dinner. Imagine!"

We listened as she told us how she'd been spending her days. There were six other sisters living with her, all from Buffalo parishes, all over the age of eighty. They prayed the rosary, went to Mass, went to confession. Last week they took a trip to the arboretum. She was also learning to play mahjong.

"What's that?" Mary Lucille said.

"Like rummy," Mother Roberta said. "With tiles. So tell me. Tell me everything. What's it like in your new life."

Therese said, "Well, we're a little out of sorts. One of the people living here—she left. She didn't like us."

"Is she safe?" Mother Roberta said. "Is she okay?" When Therese said yes, Mother Roberta told us not to worry. She was sure we had been kind, that we'd tried to impart the glory of God. That's all we can hope to do. Keep the woman in your prayers, she said. She was confident Lawnmower Jill would come back.

Before we hung up, she said, "Oh, get this. There's a wild turkey I see from the kitchen window sometimes. He comes around in the mornings. Such a weird-looking bird. Always by himself. I've named him Fred."

"How cute," Mary Lucille said.

I had been on the edge of the conversation, as if watching from far away. I said, "But how do you know—"

Everyone waited.

"How do you know it's the same turkey every time?"

"Agatha, you always ask the hard questions," Mother Roberta said.

PART II

CHASTITY

30.

The morning of my new faculty orientation, Frances made oatmeal. "It's a special day, so I put brown sugar in yours," she said, beaming. I thanked her. I ate it all.

"Good luck!" Mary Lucille said as I stepped into my shoes. "You'll be great."

"We'll see you tonight," Therese said.

It took me nine minutes to walk down Hamlet Street to the high school. I carried my textbook in a tote bag we'd bought for fifty cents at the grocery. My hair was still damp under my wimple. I was buzzing. I was alert. When I stepped in the front door, it felt as if it was the start of something, as if I could decide right then and there to become someone new. I hadn't felt that way in years.

The school motto used to be "Women by and for and with Others," but in the eighties they decided to drop the first and third prepositions and the conjunctions they required. More to the point, the principal said. "Women for Others" was emblazoned on banners and printed on pamphlets. On the walls of the gym, they had painted white over the nixed parts, so now the words were spread far apart out above the bleachers: "Women . . . for . . . Others."

"And that's why we're so thrilled to have a nun on staff again," the principal said. I was early, and we were alone together, waiting for the other new faculty members. "You've made a whole life of being 'for others.'"

I thought about reminding him that I was a sister, not a nun. Nuns were, technically speaking, cloistered. It seemed like the kind of thing he should know. But I was nervous. I just smiled.

"It used to be that we had a bunch of you teaching," he said. "Chemistry, home economics, gym. There were more nuns than regular women!" He looked at me as if I was supposed to nod; I did not. "But we haven't had a nun teach here in years. There's so few of you these days. The numbers." He shook his head. "It's a shame."

There didn't seem to be anything to say about that. He asked me to complete and sign forms that stated that my salary would go to the church, if there was an accident I would not sue, and in case of emergency they should call Abbess Paracleta.

When the other new faculty arrived—a guidance counselor, a secretary, and a biology teacher named Nadia—Mr. Ruby took us to the gymnasium, bright and big; the library; the computer lab. Then we trudged to the fifth floor to look at the chapel, which hadn't been renovated since Vatican II, when there was an influx of money, he said, when shag carpeting was something to be admired. The room smelled like old towels. At the front there was a marble statue of the Virgin Mary. Someone had put a red pack of cigarettes in her hand.

"What in tarnation," Mr. Ruby said, and then hopped with his arm outstretched to snatch it. "I've been trying to get security cameras installed all over the school, but it's a real administrative headache." He pocketed the cigarettes.

"Those'll kill you," Nadia said. It took a second for Mr. Ruby to laugh.

The tour ended at the teachers' lounge. Mr. Ruby shared the secret code in a hushed tone: 1077, the school's street address.

In the lounge there was nubby carpet, metal folding chairs, a microwave that had no clock. Seated at a card table were a few other teachers, dressed in khakis and button-up shirts. And then, to my horror, while we stood in front of the door, Mr. Ruby made an announcement. "Everyone, listen up," he said. "Listen up." My face burned as he told them our names. I remembered to smile and wave.

I'd become a member of a different, bigger team. I ducked away to stare at the water cooler. While I was filling a paper cone, the new biology teacher, Nadia, approached me. She was wearing red lipstick and creased slacks and shoes that reflected the light.

"When's your lunch period?" she said, and I told her fifth. "Mine too," she said. "Want to eat together, then, tomorrow?" and I said yes, please. Then she said, "Where's your first class? Let's go find the room."

31.

In my classroom there was a chalkboard that stretched from one end of the wall to the other. I alone had the authority to switch on and off the overhead lights. I was given a grade book and a desk with deep drawers. I had newfound powers to punish, to praise, to have the final say. I had two classes of twenty-five sophomore girls. All in all, there were two Marys and two Kates and five Katies.

The first day, I stood for several minutes while the first-period girls talked to each other. I had spent the night before thinking about what I would say to these faces, and how to say it, but when the bell rang, and I looked out at them, my mind emptied itself of any plan. They looked younger than I thought they would, and more fragile. I started with "Hello." The word sounded deranged. The girls turned in their seats and looked up at me, waiting for more. I wanted to run.

My heart was hammering away. It occurred to me there was a list of words provided to me: the class roll. I asked them to raise their hands when I called their names. I spoke extremely slowly, counting to seven between each name. And then there were no more names.

"Well, so, geometry." My voice was running a little wild. "Geometry."

A blue-haired girl named Samantha shot her hand up. "We don't know your name," she said.

A valid point: I'd forgotten to tell them who I was. Even

though I'd lived almost a decade with my religious name, I still sometimes felt inclined to introduce myself as "Isabelle." My mother's name. The name I had, too, for the first part of my life. It was a habit I couldn't shake. I didn't know if this was something my sisters experienced, too, one of those little proclivities we were too ashamed to confess to each other.

I told the girls they could call me Sister Agatha, and then I told them to get out their notebooks and write down everything they already knew about geometry. For several moments, while they moved their pencils across paper, I had some time to catch my breath.

32.

At lunch, in the teachers' lounge, Nadia drank carbonated water and ate a fresh-looking salad. I'd made a sandwich for myself with canned fish, but it had been crushed in my bag and came out looking bruised, the mayonnaise gluey. I tore off a piece of crust.

She asked how my first class had gone. Then, before I could find a way to ask her if and when and how teaching would get easier, she said, "You look like you need a donut."

I conceded: nothing sounded better. Each week after Sunday Mass, we waited, politely, patiently, until all the parishioners had taken the best donuts. By the time the laypeople had helped themselves, all that was left for us were the peanut and blueberry cake.

I wanted to choose a pretty one. I wanted sprinkles, glaze, cream filling, chocolate frosting, cinnamon sugar. I wanted the cutest, fluffiest one, waiting for me behind glass, and I wanted it warm and soft and on a paper plate, next to a white Styrofoam cup of black coffee so hot it burned the roof of my mouth. I wanted the roof of my mouth to peel off in strips. And I wanted it all, right then.

Nadia told me the lunch period was long enough we could walk to the donut place down the block.

The boy behind the counter had the kind of pimples that looked painful. He wore a hairnet and a green apron and turned to us, arms akimbo. "What will it be?"

We squatted to peer into the glass donut case. Those donuts! The cleavage of the crullers, the sheen of the glaze. Plump and full and gleaming, lined up like pageant queens. Nadia pressed her hands and nose into the glass, and it clouded with her breath.

She asked me what I wanted, and when I couldn't decide, she didn't make me. She listed donuts like the names of the saints—Chocolate sprinkles, pray for us! Boston cream, pray for us! Old-fashioned, pray for us!—and the boy bent to lift them from the case with silver tongs, arranged them on plates on a tray. I wanted to pay, but Nadia was faster with her wallet, and when I tried to hand her a dollar and fifty cents, she waved it away. I carried the tray, and then we were together at a table.

"This morning Principal Ruby gave a girl detention for laughing too loudly in the hallway," Nadia said. "I heard him tell her, 'If Jesus Christ were to return to earth and walk down this hall, He'd be offended by the way you laugh.'"

"That doesn't seem true," I said. "Probably He'd want to know what was so funny."

"The first day of school, and the man was already on a tear," Nadia said. "Ruby, I mean. Not Jesus. But maybe Jesus, too; who knows." She snuck a look to see if she'd offended me, but I smiled. She cut the chocolate sprinkles donut and gave me half. It was warm and sweet; I had to stop myself from moaning aloud.

Nadia asked me if I'd looked through the handbook, and when I shook my head, she said, "There's so many rules. And Ruby told me this year he's updated it to also outlaw nail polish and extreme hairstyles."

"What's an extreme hairstyle?" I asked.

"Um, mohawks, I guess? And blue hair," she said. "There's a sophomore girl who rocks blue hair, in my third period." Samantha, I thought. "So tell me," Nadia said. "How was teaching? It was your first time, right?"

I nodded, swallowed. "I almost passed out," I said.

Nadia gave me a sympathetic smile. "It'll get better," she said. "It just takes time. The first time I taught, I threw up." Nadia was moving on to the Boston cream; soon she'd lap me. She took a bite and handed the rest to me. It was not strange for her like it was for me, the idea of sharing food with someone you'd just met.

"Don't be shy," she said.

33.

At home I dumped the fifty-cent tote near the stairs and found my sisters in the kitchen. They were playing Operation. Therese was bent forward, easing a piece from the board with toy tweezers. No one said anything until she lifted it free, and then they all released a collective breath and turned to say hello.

"Come sit and tell us everything," Mary Lucille said. "How was it?"

"Fine," I said. "Just fine." I sat and saw they'd already plucked most of the pieces from the man's body. "What's left?"

"Funny bone, bread basket, and Charley horse," Therese said. "I'm winning right now, but it's close. You can play next round, if you want."

"Maybe," I said. Frances claimed the tweezers and stared into the man's cavities.

"So were your students nice? And did you feel prepared?" Mary Lucille asked.

"More or less," I said. "There's a lot of girls named Katherine."

I waited to see if they would ask me anything else. When nobody did, I asked, "How was your day?"

"Kind of bananas," Mary Lucille said. She waited. Everyone watched Frances pinch the Charley horse, then hold it aloft.

"Tell me," I said.

"Well," Mary Lucille said. "So the three of us walked to the community college. It was about a mile to get there—would you say a mile, Frances?"

"More. Maybe two. It was terribly hot," Frances said.

"—and when we arrived we tried to find a bulletin board to hang our flyers. We thought, college campus, plenty of foot traffic, lots of young people to recruit—"

"It's your turn, Mary Lucille," Therese said.

She took the tweezers but did nothing with them. "It's such a pretty campus. You'd love it, Agatha. All the bulletin boards were crowded. There were ads for everything: dogs for adoption, rooms for rent, tango lessons, group hikes."

"A way to cure a stutter, even," Frances said.

"The point is, we couldn't agree on a place to post our flyers. We considered pinning ours over someone else's, like other people had done," Mary Lucille said, "but that didn't seem right."

"I still think we should have," Frances said.

"But anyway, Therese had a great idea: the parking lot. We could slip the flyers under windshield wipers—more visibility," Mary Lucille said. "But first Frances and I had to go to the bathroom, and we hadn't any idea where one might be, so we approached a girl. She looked nice enough. She was sitting on a bench; she had a hoagie in one hand and a flip phone in the other."

"And I said, 'Excuse me,' and she took one look at our habits and said, 'I'm an atheist,' instead of hello," Frances said. "And I said, 'That's fine; we just had a question,' and she said, 'I don't have time,' and I tried to ask again, but she said, 'Leave me alone!'"

"She was so rude," Mary Lucille said. "Whose turn is it?"

"Yours," Therese said.

As soon as Mary Lucille started in on the bread basket, the man's large red nose lit up and buzzed. "Anyway, Agatha, we found the bathroom, and then we set off for the parking lot." She passed the tweezers to Therese.

It was then that I started to feel I'd missed out on something. This was the first day they'd spent without me in years, and I'd been so absorbed in what was in front of me that I'd forgotten about the places I could have been instead. It seemed I'd forfeited something valuable, irreproducible.

As Mary Lucille talked, I could see it all so clearly, it was almost as if I'd been there. In my mind, there we were: we walked in stops and starts, until the trees thinned out and the buildings fell away, and we arrived at a great, wide parking lot with an array of cars parked one after another. The rows stretched on forever, and the blacktop sparkled in spots where old water met spilled motor oil. At each car, we pressed our bellies to the hoods and reached to lift the wipers, and every blade, in its rise and fall, made the same two sounds: a squeal, then a slap.

I could hear that squeal. I could hear that slap.

"By the time we were done, our habits were so dirty," Frances said, "we had to shake them out like mad."

I wanted to have seen that filth fly.

"Aha!" Therese said: the funny bone.

"Then what," I said.

"Well, we saw this man walk across the lot to his car. And we watched to see if he would notice the flyer. And he did. But he balled it up and tossed it to the ground," Frances said.

"Didn't even read it," Mary Lucille added.

"He's just one person, though," Therese said. "Probably a lot of people appreciated the flyers. Probably they think it's a great idea. Frances, your turn."

Frances tried for the bread basket but couldn't get it out.

"Then we walked home," she said. "We split a Fudgsicle from the Tedeschi."

"Nice," I said, and tried to strip the hurt from my voice. I felt not needed.

Mary Lucille removed the bread basket successfully, but Therese still won.

"Want to play, Agatha?" she asked.

I shook my head. "No," I said, "I'd rather just watch."

34.

Not long after I started teaching, Baby bought a trumpet from the pawn. A way to deal with stress, he said. He used to play in high school, he said, before he dropped out, and back then he'd sold his horn for drug money. He'd hoped to buy it back but never did, and the horn he did bring home wasn't as nice. But he was thrilled anyway. He started to practice most days he didn't have to work, in the hours before dinner.

He never played whole songs. He played long chords, arpeggios, scales, and sequences, and in between he would rest, and I would think maybe it was over, and when he started up again, I jumped in my seat. I couldn't concentrate, so I went to the public library to grade and prepare for class whenever Baby had his trumpet out.

The quiet study room was available by request only, and one day the sleepy-eyed librarian told me that a man had claimed it for the rest of the month. When I walked past, I saw he had a bunch of books about becoming a paramedic, but he hadn't opened them. He was playing some sort of handheld video game.

I sat at a table near the computers and tried to read about symmetry. But I hadn't read very far when I heard someone's wacky laughter coming from the stacks.

I knew that laugh. I closed my book and went to see, and sure enough, there was Horse, sitting on the ground in the space between two bookshelves, delighted by how easy it was to rip pages from a book. She tore one free and crumpled it, stuck it in her jeans pocket and grinned, lost in private rapture.

I could tell she was seeing things I couldn't. Her blood had something it wasn't supposed to have. She was all liquid and lassitude.

"Horse," I whispered. "What are you doing?"

She stopped smiling and looked my way, but her eyes seemed to bore straight through me. "Nothing," she muttered. She tore another page, then another, with rote efficiency, but in slow motion.

"Come on, Horse," I said. "Let's go home." I reached for the book, but she hugged it to her chest.

"You can bring the book," I said. I stretched out a hand to help her up, but she shook her head, and then she kept shaking it. Her face rumpled. She looked desperate.

My sisters would have thought of something else. They would have made her get on her feet so they could see if she was in any condition to walk. Or they would have made her stand in a cold shower. They wouldn't have been so quick to let her do as she pleased. But all I could think to do was to sit on the floor and wait for Horse to excise all the insides of a book. After a while, she stopped seeing the fun in it. She told me she was ready to go home.

Horse didn't fight when Therese asked her to pee. She'd passed last Monday's drug test, but when I brought her home from the library, pale and listless, Therese took one look at her and sent her to the toilet with a tamper-free cup. Horse nodded, resigned, and the others and I stood in the kitchen to wait. Pete was in the kitchen, too, working a sudoku.

"Pete, why don't you give us a minute," Therese said.

"I'm almost done. Just pretend I'm not here."

"Go on. You can take the paper with you," Therese said.

He stalked off. Upstairs, Baby was blaring long notes that seemed to last forever.

"Shouldn't we watch her," Mary Lucille said, when Horse had shut the bathroom door, "to make sure it's her own pee she's putting in the cup?"

No, Therese said. Horse couldn't have cheated if she tried: it was hard enough for her to unscrew the top from the cup, much less do any of the things Abbess Paracleta had told us a Neon might—they might substitute someone else's pee for their own, or substitute synthetic pee for real pee, or add eye drops or Drano or dish soap. So each Monday Therese checked their pockets before they took their test, and she listened at the door and stuck a thermometer in each cup and, without a flinch, leaned close to smell each specimen before she dropped in the test strip.

Horse put the hot cup on the counter, and Therese told her to go take a nap. Horse said she wasn't tired, and Therese said she hadn't asked if she was tired. Horse tried to make sense of this, as if it was a riddle, and then Therese told her to leave.

When Horse was gone, they made me tell the story three times.

"What book was it?" Mary Lucille asked.

I shrugged. "Not sure."

"Do you remember the aisle? The Dewey decimal numbers?"

"What does it matter," Therese said.

"I'm just wondering," Mary Lucille mumbled.

Therese held the test cup to the light and watched the lines appear.

———

Therese called Abbess Paracleta. When the abbess showed up, Horse was at the kitchen table, playing solitaire. The abbess asked Therese if she could look at the test results. She glanced for only a second, and then she took a seat across from Horse, hands folded. "Horse," she said, but Horse didn't look up. She was trying to find a place for the eight of spades.

"Horse," the abbess said, firmer this time. "Do you know you failed a drug test?"

Horse nodded.

"Does the clinic know you failed a drug test?" Treatment at the methadone clinic was contingent on the patient's sobriety. "Your sponsor?"

Horse gave up on the eight of spades and picked up the jack of diamonds.

"I can call them for you, if you like," the abbess said. "Or we can go over there and talk to them together." Horse said nothing. "And you should think of where you will stay tonight."

What I liked about the abbess was that she never told anyone what they should have done. She wasn't interested in blighting anyone with shame. She dealt in procedures and plans.

There was nowhere for Horse to put the jack of diamonds, but she turned over an ace and placed it up top. The abbess said, "Horse."

Finally, Horse looked up and nodded. She looked exhausted, undone. "Okay," she said, and gently pushed all the cards into a pile and patted them into place.

She moved into an apartment in Morin Heights, in one of the Section 8 units. Pete told us she kept showing up at the granite yard for work. She was on time and did her job, as always. The two of them installed a countertop for a woman in Cranston, who had a television the size of a sofa and a sofa the size of a sailboat. And Pete said Horse did fine with the epoxy and lining up the piece right. He said she seemed happy enough: even though her new landlord was a "dick," she liked Morin Heights. She had her own microwave. The water pressure in the shower was better. She could smoke inside.

But then one day she didn't come to work.

There were rumors going around, Pete said: that she'd relapsed and been kicked out of her unit in Morin Heights, or she'd relapsed and died from choking on her puke, or she'd relapsed and was sleeping on people's front porches and fleeing before they woke up. Or she'd relapsed, overdosed, died, came back to life, and married another junkie in Atlantic City.

"Where'd you hear these rumors?" Frances asked Pete, and Pete said he never revealed his sources.

We'd lost our two women. Now Little Neon was three men and us four religious. We were supposed to choose new housemates: the abbess brought us stacks of housing applications from people who were up for parole and others who were looking to stay sober and some who were up for parole and looking to stay sober. Therese liked to flip through the stacks of paper and read the short essays. But I didn't like to look at them. They made me uneasy. There were so many applications, and just the two spots in Little Neon.

"Can I have the back bedroom?" Baby asked, when Horse left, and we told him okay, but only until the arrival of whoever came next.

35.

The girls I taught were bored and prone to naps. These concepts didn't move them—vertices and polygons and formulas. The means of calculating the surface area of a sphere would likely never overlap with the things they wanted to know about the world. They wanted to be experts in everything— cello, pinch pots, the significance of astrological signs, the hundred-meter dash, string bracelets, the periodic table, the right way to parallel park, mitosis, meiosis, French verbs in the *plus-que-parfait*—everything, everything, everything, except geometry.

I was sympathetic to this. I didn't tell them I retained nothing of high school geometry besides my teacher saying, "You're on the plane." Looking over my lesson plans, I had no real defense of geometry, except that it seemed to be our means of knowing the shape of things, and assessing our place in the world relative to everything else.

That September I told the girls everything I'd read about lines. The textbook had a whole chapter about them. A line is the connection between two points. Or three or four or however many points you want. A line lacks "curvature." It's supposed to go on forever in both directions, and it is supposed to be straight.

But here is something I know now, something I did not have the words for back then: straight is a myth. Any seemingly curveless length of graphite or ink will, upon closer inspection, reveal itself to be uneven. Think of any line from your childhood, I should have told the girls: the thick red stripe on the gymnasium floor, the skinny blue lines on a sheet of loose-leaf. Draw a line between the events of your life. Look at any of these up close, and you'll see what I mean. On earth, a line is just a bunch of bumps. There's no such thing as straight.

At night I'd lie in bed and review my lesson plans with a flashlight while the others slept. Once, I was so overwhelmed with anxiety that I shook Mary Lucille awake. "I am not meant to be a teacher," I said. "I don't think it's in God's plan for me!"

She blinked. Her face shifted and I could see that, for the first time since we'd been sisters together, she had run out of patience. "Go back to sleep," she said, as if it were easy, as if it were something anyone could do.

36.

If nonbelievers read the Bible, they would love the Bible, and if they loved the Bible, they would believe in God, and if they believed in God, they would pray to God, and if they prayed to God, whatever was broken and nasty inside them would turn tender and nice. This is what my sisters believed.

I wasn't sure it was so easy. Some people might need a little coaxing, I thought, or a little proof. But I couldn't find a way to tell them this.

At some point Frances had assumed the role of Bible study director. No one asked her to, but no one objected, either. At least, as far as I knew. I'd been more mindful lately of what I couldn't know of their time together. Sometimes it seemed our days took place in separate time zones, with their own weather. I had an idea in my head that the three of them saw a different noon than I did. But I didn't like the way this sounded: like self-pity, or jealousy. I put it away.

Frances was right for the job: she was punctual and organized and confident and did not dwell long on how she was perceived. These were her advantages in the world. I either envied her or shrank from her, depending on the day.

She compiled an agenda: introduction, prayer, lecture, read-aloud, discussion, closing prayer.

"Shouldn't we include a break? For snacks?" Mary Lucille asked.

Frances looked up from her legal pad. "All's we have the budget for is popcorn. Maybe discount chips."

"Everyone likes popcorn," Mary Lucille said. "Right?"

Frances didn't say anything, so Mary Lucille looked to me. I nodded. "Oh, yeah," I said. "People are crazy for popcorn."

Bible study was held in Little Neon's living room. Frances shut the curtains and switched on the overhead lights. Guests sat on the tattered rug, the tweed recliner, the corduroy couch, the green footstool. The footstool had one short leg, so whoever sat there spent the hour lurching.

It was mandatory for the Neons to attend Bible study, which was good, because otherwise hardly anyone would come. The first meeting, only two non-Neon people showed up, a pair of twin teenage girls I couldn't tell apart. They had been dropped off by someone in a silver car. Their mother, they told us, was making them attend. They both appeared to have crushes on Baby the instant they saw him: the swoopy hair, the hooded eyes. One cupped her hand over the other's ear and whispered something that made them both glance at him and giggle.

Frances had overestimated everything: she'd asked Father Steve to order three dozen used Bibles from his supplier in Boston. She asked for the ones in best condition, and a few copies were blank, never read, their spines uncreased. But most were pretty beat up. Some pages were yellowed out with highlighter, or full of doodles and notes. It was hard to say which Bibles made me sadder: the ones that had never been opened, or the ones that had once been loved and then given up.

Frances told Mary Lucille to pop cups and cups of corn. We had enough popcorn to fill a bathtub. It was a little burnt.

When the three of them decided to get started, Frances flicked the overhead lights on and off, like a grade school teacher hoping for quiet, even though no one was talking.

"Hello, hello, hello," she said, beaming. "Welcome. Let's start by going around and introducing ourselves. Tell everyone your name, your favorite animal, and why you've decided to study the Bible. Okay?" She waited for everyone to nod, but only the three of us did. "I'll start. My name's Sister Frances, my favorite animal is a zebra, and, uh, I decided to study the Bible because it's the best book in the world." She looked around the room. "Baby, you want to go next?"

Baby was kind and decent, but he was obligated to be bored all the time. "I'm Baby," he said, his voice flat. He was slumped low in his chair. "What else am I supposed to say?"

The twins cracked up.

Therese crossed her arms. "Your favorite animal, and your reason for studying the Bible."

"I like snakes, I guess," he said. "And I'm studying the Bible because it's required."

"I'm Tim Gary, and my favorite animal is a dolphin." He was sitting up straight, eyes bright. "And I'm studying the Bible because it's got a lot to tell us."

"I'm Mary Lucille. I love cats. And I am always trying to get to know God better."

I looked around the room. Pete brought a single piece of popcorn to his mouth, and Baby picked a hangnail, and one of the twins stared at a spot on the wall, then blew a bubble with her own spit. Only Tim Gary seemed to listen. When I said, "I think . . . giraffe, " he nodded, as if I'd made a good choice.

It took a while for everyone to talk about themselves. After, we said an Our Father, and then Therese gave a presentation about the Book of Genesis. She'd made copies of a handout: "The Patriarchal Age," it read. It was a list of the men who show up in the first five books of the Bible, with notes on each. She went through the whole list. "Noah," she read. "Father to

Shem, Ham, Japheth. Lived nine hundred fifty years, made the ark, survived the flood, invented wine."

Baby raised a hand. "Did the flood actually happen? Like, historically speaking?"

"No," Therese said. "I mean, maybe. But it doesn't really matter. What matters is more the meaning of the flood. Let's turn to it." She flipped open her Bible. "Okay. Genesis, chapter six, where God decides to punish all of humanity. Who wants to volunteer to read?"

After a painful moment of nothing, Tim Gary raised his hand. He read for a long time: about the flood and the ark and the pairs of animals and the rainbow at the end of it all. When he finished, Frances asked, "So what's this story all about?"

Pete said, "Mercy."

Tim Gary said, "Hope."

Baby said, "How God hates gay people."

I drew my breath.

Frances's eyes went wide.

Therese's got very small. "What?"

"None of the animals on the ark are gay," Baby said.

It was quiet. Then Mary Lucille said, "Well, I suppose that's true."

"Right. So the gay animals, they all drowned."

"I don't think animals can be gay," Pete said. "I think it's just a human thing."

"No, there's gay penguins," Tim Gary said, "Roy and Silo."

"Dolphins are gay," the twin on the left said.

Tim Gary looked hurt.

"Hey," I said to the twin. "Be nice." I sounded shrill.

Frances flicked the lights off and on and off and on again. "Everyone! Quiet please. Baby, you raise an interesting point. But—and while I don't think there are any bad ideas—I think maybe that's not the heart of the story. It's God's grace, right? His power along with His love."

Baby crossed his arms. "Can't there be more than one right answer?"

My sisters looked at each other. "No," said Therese.

When class was over, and it was just the four of us in the kitchen, I suggested that maybe they didn't need to start with the Old Testament. The God of the Old Testament is a very vengeful God, I said, and those stories might scare people off. I knew they wanted to get through the whole Bible, but maybe they didn't have to do it in order. Why not start with a Gospel?

"Yeah," Frances said. She seemed surprised by my helpfulness. "That's not a bad idea, actually."

Nine people felt like plenty to me, but my sisters were disappointed with the turnout. Frances said, "I realized: it's two-dollar Tuesday at the second-run cinema. That's the problem. Should we switch to Wednesdays?"

"Wednesday's karaoke night at Ick's," Mary Lucille said. "And Tim Gary works late." So we switched to Thursdays. The four of them spent the week distributing revised flyers with updated information.

On Thursday, I watched from the window as the twins stepped out of the silver car. They started to walk up the driveway, but when the silver car had driven out of sight, they turned and ran down the street in the opposite direction.

37.

From my classroom window I could watch Nadia smoke in the faculty parking lot. During her free period, she leaned against her red Jeep and lit up. On her way back inside, she tossed her butts in the dumpster, and when she saw me looking, she smiled and waved like the queen.

Nadia told me she didn't bother giving out detentions. She didn't care about any of the rules. "I can't even pretend to give a damn about whether or not my student's skirt hits her knee," she said. "Or if she wears glitter. Or if she has blue hair. What does that have to do with anything?"

I nodded. Skirts and glitter and blue hair didn't bother me, either. It seemed weird to me that anyone would look at their student closely enough to notice glitter on her eyelids, or that her skirt was an inch too short.

I was surprised by how easy it was for me to disregard the rules. I had always felt reverence for Mother Roberta's rules, and before I became a teacher—when I was younger, more ignorant of my own agency, more willing to cling to a particular way of life—I relied on commandments and codes of conduct for a sense of what was right. But Principal Ruby's rules were tedious, a nuisance, vaguely insulting. It was easier for me to act as if they didn't exist than to try and enforce them.

The students surprised me with their appetites. In the lunch-room they were greedy. Fries by the fistful, hunks of green Jell-O. Sub sandwiches stuffed with meat and cheese. Cookies in triplicate. They ate everywhere: they snuck licorice in the library and caramels on the mezzanine. They thought they were being sneaky, but I saw them try for secrecy, their jaws moving with restraint. They slipped candy wrappers into skirt pockets and between the pages of books.

And then in early October, a girl with braids nearly died after she tripped and choked on a Tootsie Roll. The Spanish teacher administered the Heimlich; the principal called the girl's parents. He also called an emergency faculty meeting after school. We met in the conference room on the ground floor, dozens of us in chairs facing the front of the room, where Mr. Ruby stood in front of a projector screen.

I sat next to Nadia. When everyone was in their seats, Mr. Ruby dimmed the lights and clicked through a slideshow of things that might go wrong in a school. Between each slide, he'd included a sound effect: a thwack, thrum, or boing.

The slideshow was extensive. He read the words on each slide: choking, seizure, broken limb, heart attack, stroke, heat stroke, fainting and loss of consciousness, outbreak of infectious disease, panic attack, fire, gas leak, power outage, hurricane, flash flood, earthquake, mudslide, bomb threat, possession of firearms, active shooting, mass shooting, terrorist attack, missing student, fist fight, sexual assault, sexual harassment, racial slurs, racial discrimination, evidence of domestic abuse, evidence of neglect, evidence of self-harm, cyber bullying, verbal bullying, death.

Mr. Ruby told us the most important thing was to remain calm in the event of an emergency. He said, "It's important to be oblivious of your surroundings."

Nadia burst out laughing, which made me laugh, too.

"Ladies," Mr. Ruby said. One of his eyes looked at me, and the other went to the side. "What's so funny?"

Nadia said, "I think you meant to say 'observant.' Or maybe you meant, 'It's important not to be oblivious.'"

"No, I know what I meant," he said, firm. "You have to be oblivious."

Mr. Ruby's assistant, a man who wore a different Hawaiian shirt each day, stood and whispered in the man's ear.

"Right," the principal said to the group. He seemed annoyed. "Like I said, it's important to pay attention to your surroundings. And remain calm."

Nadia gave me a smirk.

The principal then said if we had any concerns for the well-being of the students and staff, we could voice them now.

"The hallways and stairways," Nadia said. "They get so congested. It's not safe. We need to establish a better traffic pattern."

The principal's good eye seemed to stare right through her.

"But I've been thinking about this problem, and I might have an idea. Maybe one stairway could be for walking upstairs, and the other for walking downstairs?"

"I'm not sure that's a good idea," the principal said. "That's not in God's plan for us right now." He asked if anyone else had concerns.

I was emboldened by Nadia. I raised a hand. "Also, there's too much waste," I said, heart hammering. I asked why the school did not recycle. Plastic and aluminum were sent off in the same bins as bread crusts and orange peels, the soft stuff that easily broke down in landfills. But plastic took centuries to biodegrade. Plastic needed to be turned into something else. "Think of the impact," I said. "Think of the whales, the polar bears. Think of the earth."

The principal avoided my gaze. He said city fees for recycling pickup were exorbitant, an expense the school could ill afford.

Mr. Claude, who taught French, raised a hand. "The eating in the hallways. It's not safe."

The principal nodded. "Yes. You make a good point. That is how the girl choked. I'll issue an announcement of some sort. At once."

The next day, the principal followed through and delivered the promised edict. Over the intercom, after reciting the daily prayer of servitude, he announced: "I'm issuing a new rule, for your safety. You shall not eat in the hallways. You shall not walk and chew gum."

38.

In health class, the students learned about sex. The health teacher, Mr. Hoover, was an old man with a goatee and enormous bifocals. He liked to wear a certain sweatshirt with "Jesus is the Reason for the Season" and a full-color picture of the Nativity scene. Even in October, he wore it. The sex-ed unit was scheduled after nutrition and before first aid.

The lectures centered around anatomy. The relative positions of parts and tubes. According to their textbooks—sheepish, helpless, I snuck a look when one was forgotten in my room—sex was a diagram that could be memorized. Reproduction wasn't so different from an equation or a graph.

I knew how the students perceived me: the same as any other body lost in a habit. Prudish, callow, pure. The nuns they knew from storybooks and movies were wicked, frustrated, sexually repressed; they slapped students with rulers and had bad breath. The students pitied me, I was sure. But I remembered what it was like to be young, flush with desires I wasn't prepared to navigate. Of course I remembered.

All it took was the smell of strawberry shampoo or the give of a taffy wrapped in wax paper, and I would be privately transported to times in my youth when I'd allowed myself a little idolatry. Back then I had started to suspect it was girls I liked, since it was girls I thought of all day, in flashes: the way a spaghetti strap slipped from a girl's shoulder, or the pink of her tongue when she put a breath mint there. But I kept this to myself. I was old enough to know what a sin was. I could tell what things I wasn't supposed to think.

I know this sounds like repression. Clichéd and craven and crude. But it didn't seem like that at the time. It felt like discipline. I thought I'd overcome something, in disclaiming myself. It looked, to me, like choosing the better life.

39.

Anywhere I walked in Woonsocket, I looked for Horse and Lawnmower Jill. Every parka, every purple windbreaker, every loud laugh and scrawny woman made me think of them. One afternoon I heard the hum of a lawnmower from blocks away, and I followed the noise until I turned a corner and peeked past a hedge and could see, at last, what was making the whir. It wasn't a Bronco. It was some other massive mower. I turned, disappointed, and walked back the other way.

We prayed for Horse and Lawnmower Jill each night, sometimes aloud and sometimes in silence. I preferred the nights I could hear my sisters speak. I didn't like to wonder what they prayed for, or who they mentioned first, or whether they were more appellate or grateful or contrite.

After Lawnmower Jill and Horse left, we prayed a lot of silent, private prayers. One of the bad nights, I couldn't find anything to say to God except how sorry I was that we'd failed. I said it over and over, then crossed myself and opened my eyes. I recognized the furniture, the floorboards, the bare light bulb hanging from the rafters. There were my sisters' faces, still somber in prayer. When I closed my eyes again, I saw nothing but dark and more dark.

On good days, it wasn't hard to come up with a list of things I wanted for them. I wanted them to stand up straight and zip their coats and drink lots of water and show up on time and go to sleep without dread and find meaningful marginalia in used paperbacks. But even on those days, when the asks were easy and filled with purpose, I always preferred praying to having prayed. When the prayer was over I felt vacant, helpless to do anything but stand and walk across the room.

40.

And then there was someone new: Eileen. Therese had found her application and given it to Abbess Paracleta to approve. She was still trying to read through the rest. No one wanted to help her sort through all the paper and decide, so whoever she chose was fine by us.

Eileen, Therese told us, had been working at the all-night strip club, the one with a breakfast buffet, until she lost her job because she came to work too high to dance. She'd grown up in Milton, Massachusetts—"That's where George Bush the elder was born," Mary Lucille said—and her parents sent her to a fancy boarding school, but she was kicked out after two years. Now she was twenty-four and working at the Gap and trying to keep away from meth. She'd written in her application that she hoped living in Little Neon would help bring her closer to God.

"That's perfect!" Frances said. "That's exactly what we want!"

On a Tuesday, Abbess Paracleta brought her in the flatbed truck. Eileen was tall but fragile-looking, a hoop in her nose, blond hair pushed up in a mohawk. "I just cut it," she said, and Mary Lucille told her it was lovely.

The abbess took her for a tour. "That's the corduroy couch. No napping on the couch, and no TV after ten," I heard her say.

"I don't nap," Eileen said. "And I don't ever watch TV."

"Well," the abbess said. "In case you start."

At dinner everyone was stiff, still, polite, until the abbess said, while cutting into her chicken, "Eileen, I can set you up with GED classes, if you like."

"What does 'GED' stand for, again?" Eileen asked.

"'Get Educated, Dummy,'" Baby said.

"Hey," Frances said. "That's not very nice. Say you're sorry."

"Sorry," Baby said. Eileen shrugged it off.

"It stands for 'General Educational Development,'" the abbess said. "It's four tests that assess high school–level know-how."

"Oh, yeah, sure," Eileen said. She smiled. "Thanks."

"I know you said no last time, Baby, but it's never too late. I could sign you up, too, if you'd like," the abbess said.

"Nah. Only GED I want is a Good Edible Dinner," Baby said, and the abbess surprised us with a laugh.

41.

"Okay, it all started with a huge box," Mary Lucille told me. I was on the corduroy couch, grading homework, and the three of them came and sat next to me, looking to tell me about the massive cardboard box that was deposited on Little Neon's front steps while I was at school. "We were a little afraid of it, at first. It was enormous. Therese lugged it into the kitchen and opened it with a scissors. And inside," Mary Lucille said, watching my face for a reaction, "inside was a brand-new juicer." When I didn't say anything, she said again, "A juicer."

"State of the art," Frances said. "Top of the line. It was a marvel."

"Wow," I said. I pictured one of those giant, shiny machines that can make liquid of a hard beet or pear. A dense drum of stainless steel, and a clear dome up top where the fruit went in. "Who was it for?"

"We thought maybe Tim Gary had saved up and ordered it," Frances said, "dependent as he is on liquid meals. But we checked the label and the receipt inside and saw it was delivered by mistake." The box was addressed to a Mrs. Scrimshaw, who lived not with us at 30 Hamlet, but at 30 Hamburger, on the other side of Woonsocket.

"We also saw"—Mary Lucille lowered her voice—"that the juicer had cost four hundred dollars before tax and shipping."

"Four hundred dollars!" Therese said. "Four hundred dollars would buy a lawn mower I didn't have to push."

"Or an AC unit," Mary Lucille said, reveling in the thought. "Two AC units!"

"Or we could buy everyone new shoes," I said. "Baby's sneakers are held together with tape."

"Just imagine the Bible study flyers we could print on a four-hundred-dollar printer—glossy, bright, full color," Frances added. "Or, with four hundred dollars, we could serve pizza." She did some math in her head. "Good pizza for nine months, or bad pizza for a year."

"Oh, it turns your insides sick when you let yourself want things," Mary Lucille said.

Therese jumped in. "Anyway. The story. So we slapped new tape on the box and went to deliver the juicer." They were in the mood for fresh air, so they walked single file down the pavement in their habits and their lace-up shoes. It was cool out, but they were still sweating in their habits. They took turns carrying the box, and the cardboard softened in their fingers as they went.

They passed the trailer park and the public housing and the loan shark and the methadone clinic and the thrift. Mrs. Scrimshaw lived in a gated community just south of the private high school, where the streets were smooth and the grass perky. They hadn't seen this part of Woonsocket before. At the gate a mustached guard saluted them, safe in his little booth, and they nodded back. They walked until they found house number 30.

"It was a split-level, more brick than window," Mary Lucille said. "Gorgeous petunias out front. Mrs. Scrimshaw answered the door in a blue dress, creased in the lap."

"She looked us up and down," Frances said, "like she was appraising. And then she blew on her fingernails. The polish was still wet."

"And she goes, 'I'm sorry. I'm not interested,' and then she closed the door right in our faces," Mary Lucille said. "We didn't even have a chance to explain why we were there. And so Frances knocked again and she kept knocking until Mrs. Scrimshaw finally opened the door and Therese told her they had a package for her."

Mrs. Scrimshaw was skeptical, but she read the box's label. "Oh," she said, and thanked them. She hoped they hadn't traveled far. She stood for a moment in hesitation, and then asked, "Do you want to come in?"

They did. They elbowed each other in their rush for the cool conditioned air. Then they stood and took in the splendor.

"Agatha, you wouldn't believe it," Mary Lucille said. "High ceilings, broad windows, shiny wood floors."

"It was lovely. But the weird thing was, it was so empty. Everything in the house was missing its match," Therese said. "There was a big dining table, but just one chair, and there was a piano bench but no piano."

"And the walls were empty, but you could see blank spots where frames used to hang," Frances added. "The hooks were still in the walls."

Mrs. Scrimshaw asked them to please remove their shoes. The whole place smelled of acetone. "She offered us filtered water from the fridge," Mary Lucille said. "Or SlimFast or old chardonnay." The three of them filled their glasses with water and drank and filled them again. While they chugged, Mrs. Scrimshaw said, "You'll have to excuse the mess," and gestured to a grapefruit spoon and half a hollowed-out rind on the counter. "I wasn't expecting anyone." She blew on her fingernails and asked if, since they were here, one of them wouldn't mind opening the box. Her hands, she said, would be useless for at least an hour.

Therese said she would. They tried to act as if they didn't know what to expect, but of course they'd already had a look at the juicer. Therese poured out all the Styrofoam peanuts. When she placed the apparatus on the counter, Mrs. Scrimshaw came close and bowed before it in reverence. "Just gorgeous. It's everything I hoped for," she gushed. "Do you all drink much juice?" My sisters said they didn't, no.

Juice had many health benefits, Mrs. Scrimshaw told them, but when they asked what they were, she said she couldn't remember the specifics, but she knew she'd seen it in a headline. "She told us she was also trying to waste less produce," Frances said.

Mrs. Scrimshaw worked most days at the Pawtucket shop where girls went to get sterling studs punched in their ears for $19.95. The job left her with no energy to cook, and besides that, she had lately found mealtimes unpleasant. It was hard to cook for just one person, she said. And each piece of cutlery and china in her cupboard—wedding gifts, all—reminded her that the man she loved was at some other table, eating off some other plate.

"We gave each other a look like, wow, this woman's a perfect candidate for Bible study," Therese said.

"Forsaken women need direction, a safe haven," Frances said. "The abandoned, the sad, and the aimless—these people want someone to tell them how to put their lives back together. So I'm standing there, thinking, huh, okay, I guess God meant for us to find that juicer! So I took a flyer from my handbag and I was ready to give my spiel."

"But before we could say anything, she asked us if we had our ears pierced. She wasn't sure if nuns could wear jewelry." Mary Lucille said. "And I told her I used to wear earrings before I took my vows, but probably the holes had closed up. And she took my earlobe in her fingers—just reached out and pinched it!—and said, 'I could repierce them for you. Just wiggle an earring in, force it out the other side.' And I said uh, no thanks."

"She must be clinically depressed," Frances said. "Divorce is such a major life change. She's probably lonely, and that's why she wanted to talk to us so much."

"But she spends all day talking to people, touching their ears," Therese said.

"That's hardly enough," Frances said, "for a heartbroken lady."

"Anyway, Agatha," Therese went on, "she kept talking and talking. She told us about all the little girls who'd come in recently."

"I was waiting for a chance to bring up Bible study, but she talked for so long," Frances said. "She told us how to use the piercing gun, and the difference between cubic zirconia and diamond, and the name of the puppet she uses to distract the difficult girls."

"What did she mean by 'difficult,'" I asked, but I already knew. I could see them in my mind, these girls, who were not happy, or excited, or in a good mood. Girls who did not open their eyes the entire time. Or the ones who came in with no parent, and no permission slip, and had to be turned away. I could picture other girls, too: girls who were silent and afraid, stiff with worry, cheeks drained, on the verge of passing out; or the ones who weren't girls but infants, fragile and asleep, or else stiff-necked and howling. I imagined that many girls couldn't, wouldn't be calmed; they arched their backs and screamed so loud they were made to leave. Some would need a hard sell. Some, incentives and bribes—milkshakes, teddy bears, time with their fathers' phones. I was sure many girls said no, no, no, no, no.

"I bet they're just dramatic," Frances said. "It only hurts a second."

"Or they're rude," Mary Lucille said, "and forget to say thank you."

What if they weren't thankful, I thought. "Then what," I asked.

"She made celery juice. It tasted like refrigerator. And then at some point we invited Mrs. Scrimshaw to Bible study," Therese said. "She said she had to check her calendar, but she definitely seemed interested."

"I hope she comes," Frances said. "She seemed so . . . un-moored."

"Yeah," I said. "That's a shame." I waited to see if there was anything else they wanted to tell me. I was eager to finish my grading.

"But she's lovely, too," Frances said. She crossed her arms. "She was really nice to us."

I nodded. "I'm sure."

"It must be a nice job," Mary Lucille said, looking off into the distance, "to all day make girls happy."

42.

Two photographers—a woman with slumped shoulders who kept sneezing, and a bald man in a leather jacket who called each girl "babe"—came to take the school yearbook pictures. In third period, Nadia and I waited for our turns in the fifth-floor chapel. I watched her work a plastic comb through a knot in her hair. She'd spilled coffee on her ivory sweater, but she didn't seem to notice, or care. We were in the back of the line, and ahead of us were all our third-period students, who were peering into pocket mirrors and moving each other's hair around in preparation.

"What does one give one's mother?" Nadia said. "I have to find a gift for my mom. Her birthday is"—she looked at her watch—"well, tomorrow."

It was thrilling how relaxed she was with me, as if she didn't know I was a woman religious, or didn't care. "Flowers?" I said. "I don't know. What does your mom like to do?"

"Drink," Nadia said, and shrugged. "Whistle. Watch those shows where women take other women to the mall and tell them what pants to buy. She lives in South Boston. When I was a kid she sold perfume door-to-door. It was a pyramid scheme, I'm pretty sure. Then she married Ralph, who does something with oil. He calls me 'kid.' They go on cruises." She gave up on the knot and stuck the comb in her pocket. "Flowers are a good idea. Last year I bought her a tin of cheese popcorn."

Two more students went to sit and grin in front of the blue backgrounds, and Nadia and I stepped forward. She asked me about my mother—where did my mother live?

"Oh, she died a long time ago," I said.

Nadia's face fell.

"It's okay," I said. "It's been years." But then she reached for me, and we were hugging. Everything Nadia did was a little astonishing: it was so easy for her to do the things that scared me.

I tried to think of something to say to undo the quiet, but nothing presented itself.

"How do I look?" Nadia asked me, when it was time for us to have our pictures taken.

"Amazing," I said.

43.

Frances wanted to go on the radio to advertise the Bible study.

She called the easy-listening station in Woonsocket and the top-forty station in Providence, and both quoted her hundreds of dollars for a sixty-second ad, but the Christian contemporary station in Warwick would let her record an ad for free. Their listener count was a fraction of the other stations', but Frances couldn't say no to a deal.

Mary Lucille and Therese helped her plan. After some disagreement over the script—Frances wanted to go in an "absolutely bonkers" direction, and was being a bit of a "diva," Mary Lucille told me, when we were alone—they came up with something everyone was happy with. And then they spent the better part of a Monday in a Warwick recording studio.

When the ad was about to air, a couple of nights later, I was at the kitchen table, reading about what made polygons congruent. Eileen was across from me, solving practice reading comprehension questions for the GED, and my sisters were outside sitting in the white van, parked on the driveway with the engine on so they could listen to the radio. Mary Lucille came inside to get us. "Agatha! You guys! Hurry! It's almost time."

"Can I just wait for the next one?" I asked. The ad was scheduled to air eighteen times a week for four weeks: it would play seventy-one more times. "I have a lot of reading to do."

"But we're all together now! Come on, this is important," Mary Lucille said, and took me by the wrist. "Eileen, you too!"

In the van Therese and Frances were jittery with excitement. Eileen and I piled into the back, and Mary Lucille stepped in and shut the door.

"Can you hear back there?" Frances asked. She turned the volume up, and the last chords of a song played. Then there was the blast of a whistle, and a man began to shout. "Unclaimed fur sale!" The words were all crammed together. "November seventh and eighth at 683 Park Avenue in Cranston! Fox jackets, one eighty-eight! Raccoon vests, one twenty-eight! Mink coats, three forty-eight! Used furs! Discounted brand-new furs! Outlet furs! Furs from storage vaults and non-payment layaways! Two days only in Cranston!"

"Was that you, Frances?" I said. Only Eileen laughed.

Their commercial was next. Frances's voice came through the speaker: "What's so cool about the Bible?" and then they spent the rest of the minute supplying answers: it's hip to learn more about God; it's cool to gain wisdom; it's fun to meet like-minded people. "But wait, there's more!" Therese said, near the end. "Come to the next meeting of the Little Neon Bible Study, and you'll get one free jar of Divine Dijon mustard."

It was over so quickly. Eileen said, "Wow, you're famous!"

I said, "Hey, that was really great." I needed to get back to my textbook.

"Do I really sound like that?" Frances said. "So nasally?"

"You sounded good!" Mary Lucille said. "Do you think people were listening?"

"Oh yeah," Frances said. "It's eight-twenty p.m. Prime time!"

"I'm glad we threw in the mustard," Therese said. "It makes it more exciting."

"Yeah, that was such a good idea on your part," Frances said. "Who doesn't love free mustard?"

44.

In class I talked about the triangle. Everything good comes in threes, I said: the Father, the Son, the Holy Ghost; frankincense, gold, myrrh. In the case of triangles: angles, lines, and vertices. The girls drew triangles on the board and named them: BLT; breakfast, lunch, dinner; Beyoncé, Kelly, Michelle.

I took it all too seriously, maybe. I spoke of congruent shapes in reverent tones; how special, how beautiful, that two shapes might coincide completely when superimposed.

The students took turns tracing the outlines of each other's bodies, and then shrank them to scale. This activity was meant to demonstrate the ratio of the girl's shape to her miniature.

. I don't know what I was thinking. What kind of dolt forced a bunch of girls to stare long and hard at their own bodies, then imagine what it'd be like if they took up less space?

45.

In response to our letters to the pope, the Vatican's Office of Correspondence sent four identical envelopes with four identical slips of paper inside, thanking us for contacting His Holiness. We read them aloud in unison. "We regret that the Office cannot respond personally to every correspondence," the letters said. "However, please rest assured that the Holy Father thanks you for writing and will remember you in His prayers." We found, enclosed with the letters, eight-by-ten glossy photographs of the pope, smiling and waving at the camera, with his signature laser-printed in the corner. He had a tiny round head, a shock of white hair, ears that stuck out, a brow that was always furrowed.

"What a treasure," Frances said, and beamed at the photo. She smoothed out the creases with a fingernail.

"I've never received mail from the pope before," Therese said.

"I can't believe how quickly he replied," Mary Lucille said.

He didn't, I wanted to say. His secretary did. Any half-decent person who wanted one could have received that same form letter in the mail. I was hardly moved, but they looked so happy, so proud. My sisters—workhorses of the church! quiet keepers of the word of God!—were pleased just to be on the same planet as the pope. Their elation bothered me, though I couldn't pinpoint why.

The three of them Scotch-taped the pictures next to their

beds in the attic. I folded mine up and tucked it into my school bag.

"Oh, you creased it," Mary Lucille said, pained. "Why did you do that?"

I told her I was going to bring it to school. I didn't tell her I would slip it in a drawer where I couldn't see it.

46.

There were a number of students who worried me, who fell asleep in class or stared out the window the whole hour, but none was as perplexing as Samantha. She was as strange as she was smart. When made to answer a question in class, she spoke in a low murmur but wouldn't make eye contact—her eyes strayed out the window, or to the ceiling. She spent most class periods drawing on her knuckles, the skin of her knees, and the soles of her sneakers, with a Magic Marker. She did well on tests, and her assignments were written in penmanship that looked painful in its perfection.

One week in early October, the biology teachers made students dissect fetal pigs. Nadia showed me one after lunch: pink and stiff and sunk in formaldehyde, zipped inside a plastic bag. They'd been injected with a series of colored dyes so the students could tell the organs apart. The dissections were supposed to take place over the course of five days. I asked what they did with them after five days, and Nadia said, "Throw them in the dumpster."

Samantha was opposed to the dissection and circulated a petition to abolish the use of animal cadavers in favor of an interactive computer program that allowed students to dissect virtual frogs, but she collected only six signatures. The day students were supposed to make their first cuts into the fetal pigs, Samantha came to school in a pink, fuzzy, full-body pig costume, complete with ears and a snout. Mr. Ruby gave her detention and asked her to change into her gym uniform. She refused, and he called her mother to come pick her up. Each day that week, her mother called the school and said Samantha was staying home sick.

Nadia gave her full credit on the pig project.

I tried to make class time fun. Early on, when we learned how to calculate the areas of shapes and polygons, I brought candy ribbons and squares of chocolate and asked them to calculate: length times width. Later, they made three-dimensional shapes from toothpicks and gumdrops. In another class, they computed that the basement gym could fit 3,272 gallons of water in a hypothetical flash flood.

I worked to make them happy, but I knew nothing about the girls' lives or what they wanted. I noticed the way they talked with other teachers in the hallways; they laughed with Mr. Claude in a way they never laughed with me. In my class, they sat stiff and wordless, and when the bell rang they went to each other with obvious relief. Except Samantha. Samantha never went to anyone with relief.

During a passing period, the European history teacher, a fat man with no eyebrows, was hurrying up the stairs, head low in his focus, damp under the arms, breathing hard with effort. The stairs were crowded, filled with girls in their backpacks, and he had to charge and weave his way. At the same moment, a biology teacher, bearing a box full of fetal pigs in their sacks of preservative, was walking cautiously downstairs in order to find space for the pigs in the first-floor supply closet. So oblivious was the history teacher that he did not see the biology teacher or the box of pigs until he had collided with her, and she crashed down and the pigs went splort down the steps.

Their plastic sacs broke on impact, and formaldehyde rushed out, and little unborn pigs lay like hunks of rubber at the bottom of the steps.

Eleven pigs were lost that day. The mess it made! Girls got splashed with chemicals and had to change into gym uniforms. Formaldehyde is a horrible thing: toxic, carcinogenic, putrid. Like lacquered flesh. The smell sank into everything: the floorboards, the girls' shoes, their eyelashes, their throats.

The faculty was called for another after-school meeting. We sat close to each other in the back of the room. The principal clicked through another slideshow, this time about hallways and the use of the stairs. There were three steps to safety: LOOK, LISTEN, STAY ALIVE.

The principal said there would be a new rule: the stairways would now be unidirectional. People walking upward—from a lower floor to a higher floor—would need to walk in the north stairwell; all downward walking would happen in the south stairwell.

Nadia turned to me. "That was my idea," she whispered.

She raised a hand. "That was my idea," she said, louder this time. "And you said it wasn't in God's plan."

The principal shrugged. "God's plan can change."

Nadia sighed and slumped back in her chair, and the principal continued. "I'll announce the new rule in the morning. I ask you to enforce it strictly and without forgiveness. Students found in defiance of the rule will be issued demerits." He then looked directly at me. "And one final reminder. Giving students candy, even for the purposes of instructional activities and as prizes for achievement, is against school policy. It encourages unsafe behaviors like eating in the hallways, and endangers those students and faculty members who have allergies"—here he pointed to Mr. Claude, who raised a hand, sheepish—"and so I ask you, my colleagues, to remember this policy."

I nodded, biting my tongue, all the while making mental notes of his terminology ("endangers"!) and taking mental snapshots of the lionhearted Mr. Claude, so that later, with Nadia, I could laugh about the entire thing.

The next day I watched the students' faces as the principal announced the new rule over the intercom. "The stairwells will henceforth be unidirectional. You shall not walk up the south stairwell, and you shall not walk down the north stairwell."

The girls narrowed their eyes and turned to each other in confusion. They'd have to change their routines, the ways they went from class to class.

For many weeks the principal enjoyed a rise in popularity among the faculty. So much more efficient was the hall traffic that girls were no longer late to class, and teachers needed not penalize them for tardiness.

The girls got wise to the ways they could fill the new spare moments before the bell rang. In the bathrooms, they darkened their lash lines with the ink of ballpoint pens. They leaned against their lockers and snuck Doritos. They tossed pennies out the third-floor window and leaned forward to watch them drop. They told fortunes from folded scrap paper. I watched them meet each other in doorways, on benches, outside the computer lab, where they disclosed to each other everything they knew about the universe.

I watched them with something like envy. They always had things to tell each other.

47.

You would not believe how many people are interested in a free jar of mustard.

The week after the ad aired, there was a crowd at Bible study. Even the twin girls, the ones who usually ran off after their mother drove away—even they stuck around when they heard there was a free gift.

My sisters were thrilled with the turnout, even if some attendees were only there for the condiments. It was standing room only. There were a few teenagers and a few grown men and a bunch of grown women, maybe twenty people altogether. Everyone deposited a mountain of parkas on the kitchen table and came to sit on the corduroy couch and the living room floor and the wonky footstool. Next week, Frances told Therese and Mary Lucille, they'd have to borrow folding chairs from the parish.

"Great week to meet someone, Tim Gary," I heard Mary Lucille whisper. "So many new people!" Then, louder: "You too, Pete, Eileen. Baby. Love is in the air! I can feel it!" Pete and Eileen smiled, and Baby blushed.

"Should we wait a few minutes?" Mary Lucille asked when it was time to start. "To see if Mrs. Scrimshaw comes?"

Frances checked her watch. "Maybe she had to work."

"Maybe she's sick," Therese said.

They watched the door for a minute or two, and then they looked at each other and shrugged.

It was lucky that the week so many people showed up was the week we were discussing the Gospel of Luke. It's my favorite of the four. Luke's Jesus is the kindest Jesus, the one who's always forgiving people. And in Luke there are more women than in any other gospel. The women are healed. They're good examples. They notice things. When women see that Jesus has risen, and men don't believe the women, Jesus says to the men, "How foolish you are!" It delights me.

We discussed the Parable of the Persistent Widow, a story within a story, in which Jesus tells His disciples about a poor widow who went to a judge and pled, "Grant me justice against my adversary."

"Who's her adversary?" a woman with bangs asked, from the back.

"Like, an enemy," Pete said. "Right?"

Frances nodded. Then everyone spoke at once:

"Maybe it's her evil twin."

"I bet it's whoever killed her husband."

"Probably her evil twin killed her husband."

"It doesn't say her husband was murdered, just that he died."

"Maybe she killed him herself."

Frances switched the lights on and off. "Quiet. Quiet. Her adversary just represents whatever is harmful to her," she said. "It could be another person, sure, but it could also be, more generally, temptation, or lust, or wrath, or sloth. We don't know. We have no way of knowing. Let's move on." She continued reading: the judge refused to help the widow. But the widow kept asking and asking until she wore him down, and finally he agreed.

"What's God trying to tell us here?" Therese asked.

A lanky boy in a too-big sports jersey raised a hand. "I think it's about not being annoying," he said. "You have to respect people's wishes."

"I think it's the opposite," Tim Gary said. "I think God's telling us not to lose heart."

A girl with a lot of eye makeup put her hand up. "Right. The woman keeps trying. And then finally she gets what she wants."

"So if you ask God to avenge your ex-husband enough times," an older woman said, "He will?"

When the hour was up, Frances distributed the mustard. Abbess Paracleta had brought us a box of Divine Dijon in tiny glass jars. On the label there was an illustration of a woman in a habit, eating a hot dog with a bright stripe of mustard. "See you next week," Frances said, smiling, and placed one in every open palm.

48.

Tim Gary's birthday was on Halloween. On birthdays, Abbess Paracleta liked to take the Neons to the diner for dinner. They could have unlimited soda and order whatever dish they wanted, so long as it cost less than $15.99. We could come, too, she said; she'd just have to change the rule to $12.99.

I gave my sisters haircuts that day, the crops I knew from muscle memory: straight across on Frances and Therese, and shaggy for Mary Lucille. I cut a chunk from my ponytail, too. As we walked to the diner I kept finding new little hairs to brush from their shoulders and my own.

We walked as a group: Mary Lucille, Frances, Eileen, Pete, Baby, Tim Gary, and me. The place smelled of broiler char and ranch dressing. The sound was a maddening din: high-pitched voices, dishes clattering, and some song from the radio blaring overhead. At every table there was a kid in some getup. Babies as vegetables, children as adults—a doctor, a firefighter, a member of the armed forces—or nonhuman entities—a lion, a Frankenstein, a red M&M.

Abbess Paracleta was helping the hostess push four tables together. I sat next to Tim Gary in the middle.

The waiter was a doe-eyed young man. He told us he loved our costumes and would be right back with some waters.

"Oh, these aren't—" Mary Lucille started.

"Water. Yes. Great," Abbess Paracleta cut in, and pointed to the tent menu on our table—there was a discount for customers in costume.

We busied ourselves looking at the menu, cased in plastic, complete with high-color pictures of battered and fried foods, ribs lacquered in sauce.

The table wobbled each time the waiter set down a water. Tim Gary announced he would like a Coke. There wasn't much on the menu he could eat; burgers and pasta were too tough to chew, but he settled on tomato soup. "Tomato soup, and a big Coke."

I ordered tomato soup, too.

The abbess motioned for the waiter to bend down, and then she whispered conspiratorially in his ear.

Pete couldn't decide which TV screen he wanted to watch the football game on. His eyes kept darting from one to another. I watched him react to what he saw: his face went so quickly from hope to doom and back to hope.

Tim Gary sucked his Coke. He looked as if he might cry. And after the bowl of soup was placed in front of him, after he'd spooned it all into his mouth, after everyone's plates were cleared, Tim Gary did cry, a heavy rush of tears.

"What's wrong?" Mary Lucille said.

"Were you rooting for the Seahawks?" Pete said.

"Didn't you like your soup?" Therese said.

"Was it too spicy?" Eileen said.

Tim Gary wiped fast at his face, brought a napkin to his nose. "I'm all right, I'm all right," he said. "I just feel—it's not that I'm not grateful—it's just—"

Right then the waiter appeared and presented a bowl of pudding with a lit candle stuck in. It felt wrong to start singing, but it seemed wronger not to sing at all, so we sang at a sped-up tempo. When it was over, he wiped his cheeks and pinched out the candle.

Abbess Paracleta said, "God's given you a lot of chances in life, Tim Gary. You should be grateful."

Then Tim Gary said, "I know. I'm not—"

We waited.

"It's not that I don't like living with all of you," he said, and our cups of water shook when he set his elbows on the table. "It's just that—I am so tired of going through life alone. You don't know what it's like, never to have someone."

Abbess Paracleta told him he wasn't seeing things right. She listed his blessings: Little Neon, his health, his job, us. She quoted a psalm about giving thanks to the Lord, for He is merciful.

"And besides! I bet you'll meet someone when you least expect it!" Mary Lucille said. "Love will just sneak up on you! Catch you unawares!"

"Yeah!" Frances said. "I knew a woman who got a flat tire one day, and she called AAA, and the guy who came to fix it is now her husband! They have three kids, and a dog named Hercules! You just never know!"

Tim Gary shook his head. "You don't get it. I'm a freak," he said. "You see my face? Kids call me names." He spooned pudding into his mouth.

"Oh, the Bible is full of freaks," Therese said. She listed them on her fingers. "At some point there's a talking donkey. And Joseph's got that crazy coat. And who's weirder than Jesus? The guy could walk on water."

Tim Gary said, "Uh-huh."

Abbess Paracleta said, "You've been blessed with another year of life, because of God's mercy. It's reason to rejoice." And in that way the conversation ended. She lifted a napkin to wipe the chocolate from his mouth, then stood to pay the bill.

We were in that diner just fifty minutes. Abbess Paracleta drove off in her truck, and the nine of us walked home without saying much. How much less alone I felt, hearing Tim Gary say those things—I'd never talked to my sisters like that, never admitted to feelings of gloom. I watched him walk, head low. Pete was beside him, making conversation, but Tim Gary never once looked up.

49.

The next Friday night, to help us get in touch with the artist within, Mary Lucille presented a huge block of gray clay, wrapped in plastic. She'd bartered for it with a woman who owned a pottery studio in Cranston. I asked her what she'd given the woman in exchange for the twenty pounds of clay, and Mary Lucille said, "Three jars of mustard and a string of cheap plastic rosary beads."

Mary Lucille reduced the gray block into eight manageable hunks and gave one to each of us. She told us we could make whatever we wanted, as long as it was not in any way profane or intended to be used as drug paraphernalia.

"She's talking to you, Therese," Baby said. Eileen and I laughed, but no one else did.

I didn't know what to make. Baby was making something complicated: a teapot, we saw, after a while, with a gooseneck spout and a tiny removable lid. Eileen was sculpting a dish in which to put her retainer. Tim Gary was making a candlestick. Pete, beads to string on a necklace for his daughter. Therese and Frances were fashioning pinch pots to hold who knows what. I decided to copy what Mary Lucille was doing: she was shaping tiny figurines of religious people.

The work was wet and quiet and cold. The whole process would take a few weeks, Mary Lucille explained: we had to let them dry, then bake them in the high school's kiln, then paint them, then bake them again.

She showed me how to smooth a lump of clay into a little

figure, and she used the sharp end of a thumbtack to indicate eyes, a kabob skewer to shape the limbs. There was no patron saint of jaw cancer, so I tried to fashion Saint Apollonia, patron saint of toothache, to give to Tim Gary. But she looked more like a cocktail weenie.

50.

Baby wanted his resumé to stand out. "Maybe I should use colored paper," he said. "Orange, or blue." He was tired of working at the ice factory: "Too damn cold." He wanted to wait tables or sell discount shoes or develop film. He wanted to put on a clean shirt and a belt and go apply for jobs.

He had a hard time keeping his letters straight, so he dictated, and selected a font he liked, and I typed up his employment history.

"Okay. Ice factory. I stack bags of ice on pallets and count them. I, uh—I monitor product quality. When there's foreign objects in the ice, or the ice is yellow, or the bags aren't tied right, I fix it. My manager said I could put his name down as a reference." He told me the man's name and phone number. "And before this, in prison, I worked in the laundry room," he said, "and also the kitchen."

I didn't know how to phrase this in a way that an employer wouldn't notice or, if they did notice, would find benign.

He picked up on my hesitation. "Before I dropped out of school, I made snow cones at the mall. They made me wear a stupid hat. And I sold popcorn for the Boy Scouts, but that was only one season, because the Boy Scouts are gay."

"Baby," I said, "you have a lot of good experience. And you're so smart. But without a GED—I don't know—"

He looked at me, not unkindly. "What? I can handle it. Just tell me."

"A lot of jobs like to see high school degrees," I said, "especially if the applicant has a record."

"But the ice factory hired me."

"Yeah, but the jobs you want aren't at the ice factory."

He nodded, stone-faced.

"Baby," I said, "what do you really want to do, most of all?"

He looked at me like I was wasting his time. "I want to be normal. I want to be done with this in-between part," he said. "Not locked up, not unlocked-up. There's no word for it, really, except 'normal.'"

"You're normal, Baby," I said.

He threw his head back and sighed. "I wish I had, you know, a calling. Like you. You're *called* to do this nun thing."

It sounded true when he said it.

"You want to become a nun?" I said. "Because we'd love to have you."

He laughed, blushed, shook his head.

"You love art," I said. "You could be an artist."

"No way."

"I'm serious," I said.

"Art is for rich people. And I'm not even good enough."

"That's not true. None of that is true," I said, "You could get your GED, then go to school for it. For painting or sculpting or photography or anything. All you have to do is decide."

I studied his face as he considered it: like he'd come across a way to add whole years to his life.

The abbess was thrilled. She filed the paperwork the next day. "The GED is your ticket to a brighter future!" she told Baby. You're on the plane, I thought.

He switched his work schedule around to make time for classes, and he went with Eileen to the adult education center. The classes were self-paced. "One thing to watch out for is absolutes," I heard Eileen tell him, once. They were studying on the corduroy couch. "If one of the choices is an absolute, you can eliminate it."

Baby said something I couldn't hear.

"Anything with an extreme word, like 'always,' or 'never,' or 'only.' You can just go ahead and cross it out."

After a minute, she said, "Yeah. There aren't a lot of alwayses in the world."

51.

In November, the students' parents came with visitors' badges to talk to me about their daughters. I sat across from the mothers and fathers at a long table in the gym for fifteen minutes at a time. "Keep it brief, keep it positive, keep it rolling," the principal had advised us. "'Everyone starts somewhere'—that's what you can tell any parent who's disappointed in their kid."

These conversations were intimate, vulnerable, the closest I'd ever come to hearing a stranger's confession. The parents came with their pride, or their concerns, and in some cases, their complicated shame. They were anxious. In one conversation, a mother and father asked about their daughter's attention span—did she seem easily distracted?—and then they wept with gratitude when the answer was no, not any more so than the other girls.

Samantha's mother confided to me that Samantha was having a hard time. Other teachers had said her daughter "talked without authorization," fell asleep in class, had trouble focusing. I told her the truth: I hadn't noticed anything out of the ordinary in geometry.

Samantha was also having difficulty, her mother said, with her classmates. On the soccer field, Samantha had been called names, so she quit soccer. But the girls were still mean on the bus and in the hallways and the gym changing room, and Samantha could not avoid them.

Samantha had always been a weird girl, her mother told me, leaning forward confidingly. Always unconcerned with being like everyone else. "I don't understand it," she said.

I listened and did not interrupt. I remembered what it was like to be someone's daughter, the way a parent might look at you, all shame and rage, convinced your mission was to disgrace you both. It's how my father looked at me when I told him I was devoting my life to the church. He took it personally. He thought I was insane.

I told Samantha's mother I would look after Samantha. I told her that in my experience, there was nothing worse than feeling left out.

The parents kept coming. Over and over, I reviewed my rules, explained my policies, heard the parents' admissions of guilt and distressing observations and all-consuming fears. I didn't know what it was like, to be a parent, but I knew how to worry, and what it might help to hear. Besides, I got to know their daughters as people, not as daughters. There was a difference.

I proposed penance—ways their daughters might improve before the end of the term, opportunities for extra credit.

All was not lost, I told them; there was still time for their daughters to do well. But it was hard to look into the faces of these people a decade older than me and believe I was in any position to reassure them. "There is no time for nothing," I told them, and passed it off as if it was my own invention, as if it was something I said all the time. This was part of the way Mother Roberta had loved us: she had taught us everything and never asked for credit.

The parents were filled with resolve, as if they were the ones who'd be taking the final exam. I shook their hands and watched them go.

What work it must be, to have a daughter. My own mother, I remembered as guarded, anxious, easily distracted. I didn't want to become her. I wanted to be, as a teacher, and as a woman, some version of Mother Roberta: attentive, wise, beloved. But tough, too, the way she was—full of conviction. The sort of person you'd think about as you fell asleep, comforted to remember that in this world of bad luck and rising sea levels and impossible pain, at least, thank God, there was her.

52.

Frances saw a couple of rabbits eating the radicchio she'd planted in the backyard, which is how she remembered she'd planted radicchio in the backyard. She went outside to shoo them away and came back pink-cheeked, bearing a bucketful of radicchio heads, hardy leaves the color of wine.

I had thought Frances might grow radishes, leafy greens, carrots, squash. But because she had, months ago, planted radicchio seeds and then promptly given up on growing anything else, we now had a bounty of radicchio. We ate radicchio for weeks. We ate radicchio soup; peanut butter and pickled radicchio sandwiches; chopped radicchio salad with raisins, ham, and nuts; radicchio and eggs; radicchio on rice; radicchio radicchio radicchio.

I returned home late after my last parent conference. Everyone was asleep, and there was nothing in the fridge besides radicchio slaw and a bottle of soy sauce and four jars of mustard. I ate crackers from the pantry. When I opened the freezer to pop ice from a tray, I found—underneath the frozen peas and behind a gray lump of forgotten meat—a Popsicle in plastic.

I didn't wait for permission. I ripped open the wrapper. It was a twin-pop, purple, my favorite flavor.

Tim Gary appeared in the doorway. He looked at the Popsicle, then at me. He said, "They tried to make me a radicchio smoothie."

I split the Popsicle in half. We sat together and I asked him about his day. He told me he couldn't complain, and I said of course he could, and he said, "Okay. Well. A waitress at the restaurant, her name's Raquelle. I was—oh, I liked her. I had a little crush. She's got this long, dark, curly hair, and she's a nice girl. She's always laughing with the other guys. I just thought she was pretty. But, so, then she asked me why I was always looking at her when I was supposed to be watching the timer on the shrimp. She told me, 'Stop staring, I don't sell blow anymore.'"

I wasn't entirely sure what blow was.

"And I told her I didn't want any blow, honest, I just thought she was pretty," he went on, "and she rolled her eyes and told me I'd overcooked the shrimp."

I asked Tim Gary if it was true, if he'd really overcooked the shrimp, and he said that wasn't the point. "Just hurt my feelings, is all."

I nodded. I thought about how many more times Tim Gary must have felt glum and alone and never said anything than times he did. I pictured a pecan pie with only a single pecan taken from the top: that pecan was all the times he spoke up.

"But I'll get over it," he said.

"You have bigger fish to fry," I said, "like swordfish."

He smiled. Purple juice dripped down his arm and onto the floor. We finished our Popsicles. In the morning, Therese grumbled and took a wet sponge to the sticky spot on the linoleum. "We'll get ants, if you don't learn to clean up after yourselves," she said. "Is that what you want?" She said it as if having ants was the worst of all possible fates.

166

53.

Most days, Nadia and I ate lunch together in the fifth-floor chapel. We had the whole place to ourselves. It was much quieter than the teachers' lounge, and there was excellent light.

Nadia sometimes came to lunch smelling like vinegar. She was in charge of the photography club, and they used acetic acid to develop the film. The club met in the classroom that used to be the woodshop. They'd converted the supply closet into a darkroom, and that's where Nadia was when she wasn't teaching: agitating film in the dark.

At first there were twelve girls and only two cameras. But Nadia met with the student activities director, then the assistant principal, then the other assistant principal, then the treasurer, then the principal, and she demanded money for additional cameras. They all thought it was a waste. They told her most of the fine-arts budget had been allocated to the drama club's production of *Bye Bye Birdie*. "Poodle skirts aren't cheap," she said, imitating the principal in a low baritone, and I laughed and laughed. But Nadia was persistent. She annoyed the principal so much that he got fed up and finally okayed the purchase of ten secondhand cameras.

Sometimes we talked the whole lunch period. Other times, we didn't say much, and Nadia sat on the hardwood floor, sipped soup, graded homework, flipped through the pages of a magazine. Every now and again she'd read aloud a sentence she hated or liked. I liked to sit near the window and watch the sixth-period gym class play touch football. The girls ran about, pink-cheeked, serious. Some of them moved like gazelles, all limbs and grace, and some of them charged headfirst in whatever direction they chose, but there was one girl who didn't move much. She stayed still and watched everyone run past her and lob the ball to each other in perfect arcs, and then, arms flung ahead, the other girls went on their chase, desperate to grab the jersey of the one who'd made the catch.

54.

The week before Thanksgiving, Therese drove Tim Gary to the doctor in the big white van.

A routine exam, he told us at dinner, as we ate tuna noodle casserole. From the veins in both elbows, a nurse had siphoned vials of blood. I imagined the cold fingers of the doctor probing the soft spot where half Tim Gary's jaw used to be, feeling the contours of every last lymph node. The doctor had pressed and rubbed Tim Gary's tongue, stroked his cheeks from the inside. The tonsils were poked, the pharynx and larynx examined with a camera shoved down his throat.

"Cool," Baby said.

"Tim Gary was very brave," Therese said.

"I gagged," Tim Gary said. "I wanted to die."

"No you didn't," Frances insisted. "You don't want to die. That's why you went to the doctor."

Tim Gary shrugged. "It's just an expression," he said. He slipped a splinter of tuna into his mouth and worked to swallow.

I watched my sisters launch into speeches about the value of suffering. Frances spat off mentions of Job; Therese recited sections of Paul's letters to the Corinthians. Mary Lucille summarized parables involving leprosy and difficulties in animal husbandry, challenges that were easily surmounted with the help of the Lord.

It's true that many people could learn a thing or two from being dealt a dose of hardship, but I didn't feel that Tim Gary was one of them. I looked at the cotton in the crooks of his elbows where blood had been drawn, watched the way he lifted his straw in and out of his milk.

Mary Lucille asked him how close he was to being able to afford his next surgery, the one in which a doctor would rebuild his jaw with a piece of bone from his leg.

"Oh, I'll never be able to afford it," he said. "It's a half a million dollars, that surgery."

"Well, what did the doctor say about your jaw?" Pete asked. "Did everything seem normal?"

Tim Gary nodded. "As normal as any other jaw that's half gone."

55.

I never liked Thanksgiving. The colonialism, for one. The sad fact of the turkey skeleton sitting on the counter after the meal. There were always so many dishes to wash, and dry, and put away. Mary Lucille would get indigestion and pass gas in her sleep. I ended up so tired each year.

But that was back when every day looked like the one before. When I started teaching, my weeks took on a different rhythm, and weekends were prized in a new way. I liked my students, but teaching wore me out, and Thanksgiving was a little reprieve. The day before the holiday, I distributed pop quizzes to take up time but never bothered to grade them.

After the final bell rang, I rushed to leave. Zipped my coat, crammed my feet in boots. I had to run up to the fifth-floor chapel, where I'd left my thermos at lunch. I took the stairs two at a time.

And then at the landing I came to a halt.

In the corner, two girls were kissing. One of them was Samantha, and one of them was a girl I didn't recognize. They didn't know I was there.

My heart pounded from the climb. Everything looked a little unreal. I'd never been there at this hour: it was the first time I'd seen the light look so lovely, laid across the wall at that precise angle.

They kept kissing, eyes closed, moving their heads the way pigeons do. They slipped their hands all over each other. It was mystifying. How long had they been at it up here? I kept thinking they'd pull away from each other—surely they had to stop and catch their breath, I thought. But they didn't.

I cleared my throat.

Samantha turned her head. "Shit," she said. She wiped her mouth with the back of her hand.

"Oh, God," the other girl said. "Let's go. We're going." She slung her backpack over her shoulder. They lowered their heads and started to leave.

"I'm sorry," Samantha said, voice faint. She rushed past me.

"Wait," I said. I knew I was supposed to be the teacher, the one who had the answers, but you couldn't make a lesson plan for something like this. I felt ashamed for having found them. I had to find something to say, but it was easier to think of something to do. And I wanted to do the merciful thing.

I found my thermos under a chair and headed for the stairs. I said, "It's okay. I'll go." And I ran. I left them alone.

Later it was as if I'd imagined the whole scene. I was almost able to convince myself I'd made it up, just as I'd been almost able, when I was younger, to forget that women were what I wanted. There were so many young loves I did not consummate. I became very good at not thinking those thoughts anymore. It wasn't hard. You could learn to live without a part of yourself. You could live without a lot of parts of yourself.

I did. For years, I lived like this. And then I started to yearn for what I'd lost.

56.

I wasn't going to mention Samantha to the others, but then while we watched the weather report at night, Therese asked what happened at school that day. Keeping it from them felt like too big a lie.

"Well. I came across two girls—uh, kissing," I said. "In the chapel."

"Oh, heavens," Therese said.

Frances said I was obligated to report it. "They're young," she said. "You have to intervene when they're young, or it's a lot harder to fix. I used to know a girl who told everyone she was gay, and then her mother sent her to the right hospital, she saw a doctor, and it took years, but—it can be fixed." She smiled at me and turned back to the TV, where yellow and green blotches were moving forward and back across a map of Rhode Island.

"Don't worry," Mary Lucille said. "Someday they'll look back and be glad you helped them."

In class on Monday, I avoided Samantha's eyes, and she avoided mine. I felt stripped of all authority. I could only hope that enough time would pass that we'd be able to act as if nothing had happened.

57.

The next week I went on a field trip to the planetarium, both because Nadia asked me and because I wanted to hear what things were like on other planets.

The Providence Planetarium was in the basement of the Natural History Museum. As planetaria go, it wasn't much, but it was a bargain. Nadia said the planetarium in Boston had one of the most advanced fiber-optic projectors in the world, but in Providence a girl could get in for two dollars, and for three dollars, admission would include a packet of astronaut ice cream in one of two flavors.

The school did not spring for the ice cream.

Nadia had been teaching the girls in grade eleven about the universe—"Or," she said, "parts of it, anyway." If you chaperoned, a substitute took your classes for the day, and the gym teacher, Mr. Klamm, was filling in for me. He smiled a lot and had good posture and knew nothing about math.

On the bus, Nadia and I sat up front. The girls yelled and jeered, and when I stood to take attendance, I had to whistle to get them to quiet down. Most of the girls were girls I'd never seen, and one was Samantha. She sat alone, with headphones on.

The bus drove on a two-lane road past woods you could see straight through. I was trying to scrape together something to say to Nadia, but she spoke first. "I don't really know much more about the solar system than my students do," she said in a low voice. She'd taught herself both the biology and astronomy textbooks over the summer, as I'd done with geometry. She had finished the better part of a PhD in bioengineering, then left grad school without her degree. Now her life was worksheets. She put together lectures: she taught one class of teenage girls about the parts of the universe, and another class about the parts of the cell. She'd somehow convinced the school to let her take both classes to the planetarium. Something about photosynthesis, the sun, evolution, and life on other planets. This was not, she said, the life she'd planned for herself.

"Do you ever regret leaving?" I asked. "Graduate school, I mean."

"No one ever asks me that," she said. Instead, people wanted to know why she left. And when she told them about the thing with her advisor, they wanted to know about him. How old was he, was he attractive, was he married. Did he have tenure. Did he get to keep his job. Did he try to sleep with other students, too. Who did Nadia tell, and what did she say, and why did she wait so long.

"I don't regret leaving," she said, and sighed. "But, God. I still don't know why it took me so long. Years—years! It was hard to give up on that idea of myself."

I was too afraid to ask how to distinguish an idea of yourself from the real thing. I nodded. I watched a single orange Cheeto sail up and over our heads and land on the floor of the bus.

To enter the planetarium, we had to file down a narrow hallway past a display of stuffed and preserved red chickens, posed upright, undead. The sign said not to touch, but one bird was bald near the butt, where people had rubbed the feathers bare.

The theater smelled like feet and marshmallows and the girls clamored for seats, except Samantha, who sat at the end of the first row.

Back then, Pluto was still one of the planets. When, a year later, Pluto made the headlines and the planets went from nine to eight, I was many miles from Rhode Island, and I thought of Nadia and how she'd saved a seat for me in the planetarium, in the second row. There was an ache in my chest when I wondered if she thought of me, too.

We sat in the dark. The show started after brief advertisements for a divorce lawyer and a new kind of potato chip. Then there was fluty music, and the projector whirred, and on the screen was the whole universe. A hovering sprawl of galaxies, teeming with stars and gas and dust.

How easy it was to forget myself, to vanish, as before me nebulae glowed violet and stars flared and planets circled the sun. I hadn't expected to be so moved. Even our slim share of the cosmos, all nine planets, the way I'd always known it, was too vast to fit in my mind.

For those forty-five minutes I surrendered to wonder. It was such a relief to give up the need to be sure about things.

I wasn't sure if I should, but on the bus ride home, I told Nadia about Samantha, that I'd found her kissing another girl. I couldn't get past the idea that it was wrong. I'm not sure what I was hoping she would say.

She looked at me, waiting for more. "And?"

"And, I don't know. Is there a rule about kissing?"

"Probably. But so what?"

The way she said it, it made me feel cared for. It was like a kind of permission. She made it seem okay that I was whatever I was, too.

I looked out the window. "Yeah, so what," I said. "So what."

58.

And then it was Advent, the season of beginnings, the season of gifts. The first Friday's artist-within session, we bowed hardy pine branches to make Advent wreaths, and for days our fingers were tacky with sap. We sold the wreaths to parishioners and gave the money to the rectory. Each one was sold, taken to brown on other people's kitchen tables, and we were glad to see them go.

The boiler in the basement of St. Gertrude's had been around for forty-eight winters, since before Vatican II. It was a complicated thing, and real temperamental. It got easily worked up and then had a hard time calming down. At night, Father Steve kept the doors of the church unlocked, the heat blasting, so people who needed to could come sleep in the pews.

The morning of the Immaculate Conception, we went to Mass first thing. It was a Thursday in early December, and the world was still dark. Only Tim Gary came with us; the other Neons stayed in bed. We sat in the front row, like always. When the bells rang, we startled. We were struggling to stay awake. The heat made us drowsy; we hadn't had coffee; we bit our tongues and pinched each other's elbows.

There were no more than ten people in the pews, even though it was a feast day, a day of obligation. The Mass was intended to celebrate the miracle of the Virgin Mary getting made: that Saint Joachim and Saint Anne loved each other and made a little sinless embryo that'd become a sinless girl who'd grow up to become the sinless womb in which the Lord gestated, the sinless womb from which the Lord came crying.

He read from Luke: the Annunciation, the moment when Mary is told she's pregnant with the son of God. Father Steve seemed emotional; his voice broke when he read Mary's consent, the last words of the passage: "Behold, I am the handmaid of the Lord. May it be done to me according to your word."

The homily was about abortion. Father Steve called it genocide. He invited everyone to join the group of parish members who drove to the women's health clinic in Providence each Saturday to pray and stick signs in the ground and hand out pamphlets.

"Let's join them," Mary Lucille whispered to us.

"Of course," Frances said, and Therese nodded without turning her head.

Maybe that's when I started to wonder about their priorities, the ways they wanted to spend their time. But it might have been earlier. Either way, it was a relief that I didn't have to come up with something to say. I knew I was supposed to agree with Father Steve and my sisters, but I was thinking of my mother, and the times I rubbed her swollen ankles when she was pregnant with my brother. How she'd been made to feel cruel to want anything other than her lot in life. And I was thinking of mercy, how it can make gravity lift, so sinners float awhile, and every fallen leaf returns to its mother tree and is welcomed back to the branches of the living.

The sun had risen by the time we stood to receive Communion, and it poured through the stained glass and made everything glow.

59.

I slipped dozens of Scantrons into grading machines, listened to the wrong answers go click click click click click. And then my first semester was done.

I had two weeks in which to learn the second semester of geometry, which was all congruence and proportionality and ratios. But I could only read the geometry textbook for a few hours a morning, or I turned irritable. It was hard to know what to do with all the rest of my time. I listened to Therese practice her lecture for the next week's Bible study, about the Book of Esther. I soaked and boiled beans. I went walking and kept walking.

Our sculptures came back from the kiln, some in pieces. Frances's pinch pot was broken in half, and Mary Lucille's tiny Christina the Astonishing had exploded into a thousand pieces. Mary Lucille accepted the news stoically. She had already successfully made, she told me, a half-dozen figurines, each the size of chess pieces. She hoped to sell them in the parish gift shop.

My cocktail weenie had cooked without breaking, and I painted it, which required my utmost concentration, the slightest and most tender of brushstrokes: the pink mouth fine as thread, the wee fingers and thumbs. I hated the wee fingers and thumbs, but otherwise I enjoyed staring at the weenie and deciding what to do to make it look like something else.

I spent a lot of time that December thinking about resemblance, the fraught relationship between a thing and its copy.

The little people Mary Lucille and I made were all replicas, some ugly, of unknowable originals. We could get only as close as the copy, and the copy was never enough: her miniature Joan and Catherine and Clare stood all day in the gift shop display case. They did not speak or perform miracles; they only gazed out all day from behind glass.

And they did not sell, much to her resentment. Deacon Greg told her no one had any need for knickknacks. "You could brew kombucha," he said. "A growler of kombucha makes a great gift. Very popular. Or you could knit socks. Things people actually use."

But where was the good in making things that would not last? I wanted to create things that would outlive me. I wanted to pay homage to the women I admired: Quiteria, who was beheaded after she refused to marry a man; Lidwina, who ice-skated; Hildegard, who knew her science. And Apollonia, who'd had all her teeth knocked out by a mob of people who didn't believe in God.

When by accident Mary Lucille made a blue-faced Virgin Mary (she'd missed the edge of the veil with her brush), she gave the figurine to Mickey, the cashier at the Tedeschi. By then, Mickey was eight months pregnant with a baby she did not want.

Mary Lucille told her, "Mary will watch over you and your child."

Mickey said, "Mary looks like she's queasy at the thought."

Mary Lucille said she probably just had a little morning sickness.

Mickey looked at the little face. She said, "Poor Mary. She didn't even get to fuck first." She placed the Virgin on top of the cash register.

60.

The day it snowed eight inches in Woonsocket, the four of us found Lawnmower Jill slumped in the alley behind the library, her mower parked beside her, a white plastic Tedeschi bag in her lap. It'd been months since we'd seen her last.

"Lawnmower Jill!" Frances called, but she didn't lift her head.

When we knelt next to her, Lawnmower Jill roused and asked us, "Sisters, how does the zebra escape from the belly of the wolf?"

We shook our heads; we did not know. It was a few days before Christmas, and Woonsocket was gray and coated in ice. Lawnmower Jill wiped her pink nose with a chapped bare hand.

She told us: "Limb by limb."

Frances reminded Lawnmower Jill that wolves did not usually eat zebras.

Lawnmower Jill said, "What about a little baby? How do you know wolves don't eat the zebra babies?"

We confessed: it was possible. Who could say what went on in the belly of the wolf?

Lawnmower Jill was drunk on Narragansetts and high on something we couldn't name, but this didn't make her observation any less true. Every escape happens one inch at a time.

Therese said, "Where are you living these days? Let's get you somewhere warm."

But Lawnmower Jill ignored her. She told us she had good news. She had just been hired to sell jewelry. When we asked where, she said, "The jewelry store." Tomorrow would be her first day.

We knew of no jeweler in Woonsocket. In Woonsocket there were no jobs for people looking, but it didn't matter, because the people didn't look.

Therese said, "Which store?"

Lawnmower Jill said, "A new one. Brand-new. Sisters, will you help me find something beautiful to wear?"

We were glad to see her, but we had a million errands, Frances told her. We had to do a million things.

Lawnmower Jill cocked her head. "Like what?"

"Church business," Frances said. "We have to shovel the parish driveway." There were also private matters: we needed to buy antacid at the Tedeschi, explain our way out of Blockbuster fees, pick up prescriptions, get a new light bulb from the hardware store. "Maybe you can come over for dinner one day soon," Frances said.

Lawnmower Jill rolled her eyes. "Let's go," she said, and stood to straddle her mower. "I'll help you shovel the driveway if you help me with a dress."

We hated the snow and we hated relocating it. Lawnmower Jill, tall and strong as she was, could clear it all with ease, we knew. And so we nodded, said that sounded fair.

"But you can't drive," Mary Lucille said. "You're in no state."

When Lawnmower Jill smiled, it seemed she was trying to give each yellow tooth some air. "I'm in my best state, Sisters," she said. "Meet me at the thrift." She fired up her lawnmower, and the dashboard glowed with a constellation of warning lights that went out one by one.

She picked first a dress of velvet, and we said, "Velvet's hard to clean."

The cotton was too sheer; the poplin had a hole.

We showed her blazers. We brought blouses with collars and bows.

"Too stuffy," she said.

Then we found, in a crowded rack, a shift dress in navy nylon. Knee-length, with flattering seams at the waist and bust. There were chalky rings around the armholes, but that was nothing a soak couldn't fix.

We knocked twice on the changing room door. Mary Lucille said, "You're going to like this one." There was no response.

Frances said, "It's perfect. Here, look."

When at last she opened the door, Lawnmower Jill was in a sequined dress: sleeveless and covered in a million twinkling coins. She grinned; she twirled. Below the hem, her calves were sallow and spotted with scabs, and the dress's waist was inches too generous, her slight form overwhelmed. But when she turned and considered herself in the mirror, it looked as if the dress had healed something deep within her, and the sequins launched beams of light around the room.

She said, "Isn't it something? Isn't it special?"

Mary Lucille was the first to gush. "Oh, it's lovely."

Frances said, "I'm a little worried you'll outshine the diamonds."

Lawnmower Jill smiled. She said, "I don't have any diamonds, sister."

Frances said, "The diamonds at the store."

There was a moment, then, when we could see her story catch up to her, like a shockwave of recognition that ran through her skeleton. "Yes. Yes, you're probably right."

The dress went on glittering. Frances said, "Do you really have a job?"

Lawnmower Jill's face went wild with hurt.

Frances said, quickly, "It's okay if you don't."

Lawnmower Jill crossed her arms and said, voice caustic and rushed, "Who told you what's okay and what's not?"

We looked at each other. Mary Lucille said, "I'm sure Sister Frances didn't mean to upset you. It's just we miss you. We miss you and we want to make sure you're okay and we're sorry you left Little Neon and we love you and we pray for you all the time—"

Lawnmower Jill's eyes sped up and her neck flushed over. She grabbed her plastic bag from the changing room floor. She rushed past us, and we watched her go, headlong through the denim aisle, past the display of snake-like belts. She did not stop at the register, and she did not pay for her sequined frock, but went on, and wore the dress right out the doors, which parted for her and stayed wide long after she was out of sight.

We went with our purses to pay at the counter.

When we walked back from the thrift, we thought we might find Lawnmower Jill parked behind the library like before, but she wasn't there. It had started to snow, big wet globs that fell fast. Probably, we agreed, Lawnmower Jill was by the old drawbridge, or in a parking garage, or drinking the free coffee at the bank.

As we walked, Frances asked me what ever happened with the two students who were kissing.

"Oh, it's out of my hands," I said. I stared at my feet as I walked.

"So you told someone about it," she said.

"Yeah," I said. "I did." And this felt like the truth.

Inside the Tedeschi, we found Mickey, eating fat cheese puffs. Her red apron hung over her big belly.

Mary Lucille asked Mickey how she was feeling, and Mickey said she was feeling like shit. She still couldn't keep her breakfast down and she couldn't take her Ritalin and at night she couldn't sleep.

Frances asked her, uneasy, if there was anything we could do.

She licked a fingertip and said, "Yeah. Cover the register while I pee."

Kindness isn't any good if there's no follow-through, so even though we didn't know how to work the cash box or distinguish between types of tobacco, we stood before the cigarettes and the lotto tickets and looked out at the aisles. Dark pop in big bottles, beer in tall cans, white cartons of milk. Shelves stacked with bagged candy and nuts, and a million varieties of chips and jerky. We smiled to see, standing upright on the cash register, the Virgin Mary statue Frances had made. She looked calm, staring back at us.

A bell rang when the door opened, and we looked up to see Horse. She lurched in, wearing her purple windbreaker, and flung back her dirty hood.

"Horse," Therese said. "Have you seen Lawnmower Jill?"

She shook her head. "Last I saw her, she was behind the library." Then Horse asked for Mickey. She told us, "Most days, Mickey will sell me a tall boy and a bag of Fritos for a buck."

"And what about the other days?" Frances said.

Horse said on the other days she got her beer somewhere else. "But when Mickey's here, she does right by me."

We looked at Horse, and we looked at each other. No one

could say if what Horse said was true, but either way we knew she wasn't supposed to be drinking beer. I offered to buy Horse some peanuts, but Horse didn't want my charity. She wanted nothing to do with us. She said we were a bunch of cunts, and she left without saying goodbye.

When Mickey came back from the toilet, we stepped away from the register and in the aisles bent to find antacid. We also grabbed a pouch of peach rings and a liter of root beer.

"Anyone come by?" Mickey asked, guiding the bar codes across the laser.

We might have bragged to her about how tough we'd been, about our refusal to let the Tedeschi name be sullied. But we didn't want to draw attention to our good work. Gloating's an ugly thing. And so we told her, "No one special."

Mickey winced at something internal, rubbed her big belly. Therese handed her some money and put the bottle of antacid in her coat pocket.

The little bell rang when we opened the door, as if to signal that the best part of any place is the door, and the best part of any door is the other side of it. We stepped into the gray day, the snow shin-high.

Snow kept falling as we walked to Blockbuster, and we spoke in hushed tones about Lawnmower Jill. No coat, no gloves, no snow tires—we vowed to make sure she was somewhere warm before nightfall.

We pulled our parkas tight and kept our eyes and noses low. We knew a trick for walking in the snow. You have to make each step deliberate—plant it hard—and put your foot where another foot has already stepped. We trudged single file, leaving only one set of prints.

In order to have our late charges forgiven, we needed only to speak kindly to the Blockbuster girl. We knew her from Mass. She sat with her parents and her five siblings in a pew near the front and liked to chew the end of her braid. We promised we'd watch the movie we'd rented—a documentary about pandas—and return it by the end of the week.

When we asked the girl if she'd seen Lawnmower Jill, she said she'd seen her in the library the day before. But she wasn't supposed to talk to Lawnmower Jill; her parents had told her to keep away from junkies.

Mary Lucille's fingers were bluing, and Frances and Therese were cranky (cold toes and hunger, respectively), so I volunteered to pick up a light bulb at the hardware store while the others went to the pharmacy.

There might be women out there who can stand to hear other people complain for hours on end, but I am not one of them. I love the snow. I love the hardware store. It is easy to forget one's need for these things: fresh air, time spent alone.

There were so many light bulbs to choose from: round and globular, narrow and pointy, a big range of watts and volts. What number watts was right? I went home with six different bulbs.

I walked in the snow, the cold a numbing agent. When I met up with the others, we didn't have time to talk about the light bulb; we saw Horse on the top step of the Tedeschi with four tall cans of beer standing upright in the snow.

"Horse," Therese said.

"It's you guys!" she said. She seemed to have forgotten we were cunts.

"That's a lot of beer, Horse," Frances said.

Horse grinned and said, "Mickey's little baby's coming."

Therese said, "No, Mickey still has a month to go."

Horse shook her head and issued a laugh that suggested she had only a loose grip on the events transpiring before her.

Inside, Mickey was bent over the counter, her face pressed into the laminate.

At first, we were gentle and sweet. "Are you in labor?" Frances asked, and Mary Lucille stroked Mickey's hair.

Mickey could only howl.

And then we were no longer sweet. Everything announced itself to us with urgency: the droop of Mickey's wet pants; her lips, pale and raw. Our knowledge of birth came from the movies. About the pain, we asked how long, what kind, how big, and her answers came as moans. I pressed the artery in her wrist and counted its swell.

When we told Mickey we'd better take her to the hospital, she opened her eyes and seemed to notice us for the first time. "Sisters," she said. "Am I gonna die?"

The ambulance dispatcher reported that Woonsocket's ambulance was stuck in the snow. "Try a cab," the operator said. "Or a friend."

Empire Cab, Orange Cab, Island Cab, and Mr. Taxi quoted Frances hourlong waits. "Eight inches of snow, honey," one of the men told her.

Mickey spat swears like seeds.

And then we ran to the door to see the indomitable vehicle charge down the sidewalk, bright and brave and undeterred by snow: the gleaming orange lawnmower, and oh, yes, perched upright on the seat, gallant and brilliant in her sequins, was Lawnmower Jill, her bare arms pink. We watched her come to a stop outside the Tedeschi, and Horse handed her a beer.

We each hurried to grab a limb and proceeded to carry

Mickey hammock-style out the door. The bell clanged its jolly clang and to Horse, we said, "Move," and to Lawnmower Jill, we yelled, "Baby's coming!"

One of us slapped the new beer from her hand. Lawnmower Jill said, "Fuck," and we said, "Let's go." There was no way the four of us could fit on the mower, so we planted the wailing Mickey atop Lawnmower Jill's lap.

Dread and panic swept across Lawnmower Jill's face. She shook her head, but we nodded back. She said, "No, no, no," and we said, "You must, you must, you must."

We said, "The hospital's just three miles down the road."

She said, "Sisters, that's way too fucking far."

We said, "Just take it one inch at a time."

Something shifted within her, as if a seam were pulled taut. She released a breath and a final curse, and then took hold of Mickey and started her engine.

We could see that this didn't thrill Mickey—she issued a curse of her own—but surely she would soon find reason to smile. And oh, the stories she would tell her little baby about this day. How lucky, how blessed she was, that Lawnmower Jill had come along.

We stood back and watched them tut down the sidewalk. The mower sent out clumps of thick exhaust and, as it went forward, pushed through the soft snow where no one had yet walked, leaving behind thick tracks in the blank belt of sidewalk frost.

For the rest of the night, many hours after the store was scheduled to close, we stayed behind the counter under the bright lights of the Tedeschi, eyeing and pleading to the little blue-faced Mary atop the register. Horse was asleep in the corner, and every ten minutes we would lift the receiver from the phone on the wall and call the birth ward and ask to speak to

Lawnmower Jill. "Any news?" we'd ask, and Lawnmower Jill told us there wasn't any news, until there was—Mickey birthed a boy, Lawnmower Jill said, a loud, gooey thing they wrapped up and gave a little hat.

We shook Horse awake to tell her the news and left her belly-up and drooling in the unlocked store, and in our glee we walked home, side by side, gloved hand in gloved hand, four across. We kicked into the gathered snow, which glittered in the moonlight. We had the keen feeling that everyone, at that moment, was safe, even the rodents, nestled underground, and though it wasn't the case, we had no reason to believe we would ever suffer again. It's easy to be fooled by joy, to think it will never abandon you, never leave room for hunger and fear.

Under the highway overpass, we shrieked to hear the echo, and we waited until the last memory of our voices had died. And then we turned the corner and arrived at our little street.

If I had a pulpit, I would preach about driveways. Our short black link to the unknown, our supremacy over the grass. We think we've memorized their every inch—the fist-big crack, the belt of tough tar, the place where the lawn begins.

But imagine my surprise, I'd tell my disciples. Imagine my shock when we plodded up to our house and found the thick tracks of the mower's wheels pressed in the sidewalk snow. Imagine how stunned and small we felt when we saw that all the snow in our driveway had been cleared away. A million flakes, lifted and thrown by the shovelful, so our walk to the door was made easier, so we could see, through the sparkling rime, all the dark pavement beneath.

61.

Here's what I remember of Christmas: a week before, we sent cards to Mother Roberta, our families, Father Steve and Deacon Greg, the pope. From the garage, Tim Gary dragged in the plastic tree that Little Neon kept decorated all year, covered with a bedsheet to keep off dust. Christmas Eve, Mary Lucille sliced her thumb cutting onions. The lasagna was too salty. The ice cream was peppermint.

After dinner, we gathered around the speakerphone to call Mother Roberta. She told us that in Buffalo, the bishop had announced more cutbacks. Elementary schools would close, parishes would be consolidated, and more sisters like us would be sent away. At least seventeen sisters had been invited to retire early and would soon move into the home where she lived.

Not a very good plan, in Mother Roberta's opinion. Not her idea of a long-term solution. "It's ugly, the way they're handling things. Claptrap. What the diocese needs to do," she said, "is file for bankruptcy." She hacked something up from her throat. "If I were in charge—" But she didn't finish the sentence.

62.

January I was back to school, in thick tights and heavy sweaters.

Here's a little word for an overwhelming concept: pi. The time had come for me to teach it. There are many ways to talk about pi; I chose to list adjectives. Pi is irrational. Transcendental. A mathematical constant.

They had a hard time with it. One girl wanted to know how pi could have an infinite number of decimal places. She asked, "What does it mean, exactly, for the digits to go on and on forever?"

Forever—I'd forgotten how stressful a concept it can be.

I told the girls everything I'd read: Pi is a perfect idea but not a perfect number. You could list digits of pi for the rest of your life and still have failed to calculate most of it, because its digits went on and on, forever, without end. The more computing mathematicians did, the more digits they were able to list, the closer they got to perfect, I said. But they'd never finish.

Samantha asked me, "But what's the point? They'll never figure out the whole thing, so what's the point?"

I told her looking for the point ruins the fun. "Cultivate your ability to forget about the point," I said. I tried to explain that work could keep a woman upright, so long as she didn't look for the point. The slow unfolding of progress—this was enough. Work begetting more work.

Infinity, I told the girls, is a state of boundlessness, which is both terrifying and full of hope. "Just like God," I said. The girls blinked. They did not write this down.

"Maybe," I said, "we don't have the right words to talk about these things. I can tell you what infinity is like, but I'd be using my own words. And I only have so many words, not an endless number, an infinite number of words."

I could see I was losing them.

"But anyway," I said. "Pi. Let's look at how it begins. And how we can use it."

I erased the board very slowly, then erased it again. This bought me some time to myself.

63.

February: the deep, bleak void of the year. We were familiar with its mercilessness. Lackawanna Februarys had been devoid of wonder and ease, and the same was true in Woonsocket. We relinquished joy. We barely spoke. We did not smile. Not once did we clean the toilet on the second floor.

The fates of our houseplants were not ours to determine; our pothos atrophied and our hardy mums shrank. When we watered them, the water froze in the dirt.

So we gave in. We sealed the windows of every room with gray felt. The four of us pushed our beds together to sleep close, under blankets that plugged into the wall. We spent whole evenings sitting on the kitchen floor before an open oven with Baby and Tim Gary and Pete and Eileen, playing cards, or doing nothing except waiting to be warm again.

Valentine's Day, Pete went to Cranston to sit with his daughter and a supervisor in a room with windows for walls. He told us he brought his daughter chocolates. He'd made her a card, too, and included lines from an Anne Sexton poem: "a small milky mouse / of a girl, already loved, already loud in the house / of herself." The girl read the card and looked over the box, then informed him she was allergic to nuts.

"What'd you do with the chocolates?" Mary Lucille asked.

"They're on the counter," he said.

"I'm sure she appreciated the card," I said.

Pete shrugged. "Her mom got her a five-pound gummy bear,"

he said, "which is equal to fourteen hundred regularly sized gummy bears."

"But how do you eat it?" Mary Lucille asked. "With a fork and knife?"

Pete shrugged.

After a moment, Baby: "Anyone want to go to a meeting?"

Pete nodded and said that was a good idea. Eileen said yeah. Tim Gary shrugged and said why not.

"There's one at the community center on South Main; starts in twenty minutes," Baby said. Then he looked at the four of us. "It's cold—can we get a ride?"

So everyone put their dishes in the sink and piled into the white van. The streets were slick, so Therese drove slowly, hunched up at the wheel. When we pulled up outside the building, everyone piled out, and Baby shut the van door.

"Should we go in, too?" Mary Lucille asked.

"No way," Therese said. "It's private."

"Well, we can't wait in the car," Mary Lucille said. "We'll freeze."

"We can keep it running," Therese said.

"That's wasteful," I said.

"We'll go home and come back," Frances said.

Therese shook her head. "We'll have to turn right around by the time we get home."

Mary Lucille rolled down her window. "Baby!" she yelled. He turned. "We should go home, right? And come back?" Baby nodded as if it was obvious. Then he disappeared inside.

64.

Where we lived, there was a fox. A sleek, gorgeous thing with a tiny face, upright ears, quick legs. It did not hibernate; foxes don't. It spent all winter aboveground. From the sofa, drinking coffee, we liked to watch it slink through the snow in Little Neon's yard each dawn. It looked scrawny. It made me think of Mother Roberta's turkey: it's possible there was a whole group of foxes, a whole skulk, but we never saw more than a single fox at a time, strutting on its own, and so we chose to believe there was only the one lone brave fox. Mary Lucille left it cans of hot dogs behind the oak tree.

On Ash Wednesday we woke at dawn to be blessed by Father Steve at the parish. In February, dressing was an act of assuming more and more space: thermals, sweaters, fleeces, parkas zipped to our chins. We drank coffee in fast slurps, and then laced our boots and crammed our hands into mittens only after we'd fastened and tucked ourselves away and locked the door.

On our way to church, Mary Lucille stooped to set an open can of hot dogs in the snow. Ash Wednesday was the last time she made an offering, because Tim Gary found the Ash Wednesday hot dogs.

He confronted us, and when we explained what the hot dogs were for, he fumed. What were we thinking? How could we lure such an unkind creature—a predator—to our yard?

We were sorry, Therese told him. "We were only trying—"

"Go to the store and buy a raw chicken."

Frances was quick to say we would. We walked to the

Price Rite and bought the biggest chicken we could find. Seven pounds, wrapped airtight, cold and dense.

When we presented it to Tim Gary, he did not thank us. He didn't say anything at all. He was in the yard, whistling a tune we didn't know—something slow and melodic. He ripped the plastic free. The chicken was luminous, like a big, misshapen pearl. Tim Gary, still whistling, chucked the wet meat into the back of a metal box trap, no bigger than a Weber grill. He set the trap next to a bush, and then he went inside to wait.

Hours passed; evening gave way to night. Pete asked Tim Gary what he was going to do once he'd trapped the fox, and Tim Gary said, "You'll see."

After curfew, in the attic, we unfastened our habits and freed our feet from our pantyhose and hung up our veils. Outside there was clatter, and we went to the window to see Tim Gary on the grass, laughing and clapping his hands. That's when we saw the fox, trapped in the cage with the gleaming chicken. Tim Gary knelt in the snow to mock the fox, jeering in a nasty way, and we thought for a second that the fox might attack him through the bars of the cage, but then Tim Gary stood and carried the trap around to the garage, where we could no longer see, but we heard the groan of the garage door as Tim Gary made it rise and fall, locking us in the same house as the fox.

Panicked, we ran down in our nightclothes and bare feet. We expected to find gnashing jaws and wild eyes, but the fox looked shrunken and weak in its cage.

Tim Gary turned on the garage sink and pulled the nozzle so the water ran into an empty trash can. The hose twitched as the water came rushing. He let it run until the trash can was full.

Mary Lucille asked, horrified, "What are you doing?"

Therese said, "Tim Gary, it's past curfew!"

He didn't answer. He offered no explanation, no confession, no plea or defense. He only picked up the cage, and the fox trembled in the air. We watched the animal shake and seize.

"Stop it!" Frances yelled, but then all at once Tim Gary plunged the cage into the trash can. Water went flying, but there was enough left to engulf the fox until its trembling stopped.

Tim Gary breathed hard and turned off the sink. His gloves and the sleeves of his flannel were sopping, and he was red in the face.

"What is the matter with you?" Therese yelled. "That was—so—so—"

"Cruel!" Frances said.

"Oh, the poor fox," Mary Lucille said, and I saw that she was crying. "One of God's creatures!"

"Tim Gary," I said. "Wasn't there another way?"

"Had to happen," he said, and we repeated these words to ourselves later, after he'd disposed of the carcass, after he'd scrubbed his hands with steel wool until they were pink and raw.

We locked ourselves in the attic and for a while sat stunned and afraid. We acknowledged aloud to each other that Tim Gary did not seem okay.

"I saw him looking in the personal ads the other day," Therese said, her hands folded on her lap. "He had a pen in his hand, but he didn't lift it once."

"The personal ads are on the same page as the crossword," I said, impatient. "He was probably just doing the crossword."

"I think it's SAD—seasonal affective disorder. He's depressed because he doesn't get enough vitamin D," Frances said. "The socks he was wearing today, he's worn every day this week. The same pair."

"Last Tuesday I saw him eating pudding with the lights off," Mary Lucille said, leaning forward to whisper. "It was nine-thirty at night. I turned the kitchen lights on and he said, 'I don't want them on.'" She made her can-you-imagine face.

I recognized this side of them. In Lackawanna they were always jockeying to be the most loving woman at the day care, the one the babies liked best. Here they were, lobbing their theories, casually competing to see who had the most insight, who had been watching Tim Gary most closely. They each wanted to be his earthly savior, and it seemed as if it wasn't for Tim Gary's sake, but for their own, because they liked the way it made them look.

65.

Things turned, or seemed to, when winter gave way to warmer weather. The stupid snow melted quickly and left everything muddy and soft.

The first Saturday in March, Baby and Eileen both passed the GED. Mary Lucille made brownies. "I undercooked them," she said, proud, "so they're still like fudge inside."

"It's not that big a deal," Baby said. "Something like eighty percent of people pass."

"Speak for yourself," Eileen said. "I barely passed."

"Passing is passing," Baby said. He was going to apply to new jobs, he said. Finally leave the ice factory behind.

I wanted to make changes, too. For Lent, the season of sacrifice, I made a list of things not to do less often, but to do more. I wanted to fit in two additional rosaries a day, start taking multivitamins, and help Tim Gary. Give him a way to shore himself up.

Mother Roberta used to say all a person needed was somewhere to go and something to do. From the kitchen window I studied the abandoned apiary in the backyard. Maybe Tim Gary needed to have bees again.

And so one weekend I sat in front of the St. Gertrude's computer and found the rudimentary website of a man in Hopedale, only twelve miles north of Woonsocket. He bred honeybees and sold them in boxes of twelve thousand.

I dialed his number. When the apiarist answered, he sounded impatient, as if he'd been pulled from pleasure by the ring of the phone.

I told him I was a customer intending to buy bees. I was interested, I said, in the Carniolans—tough, resistant to mites. "But I have a quick question. How do I get the bees out of the box without getting stung?"

He explained that all I'd need to do is throw the box on the ground, wiggle free the lid, and pour out the bees. They'd spill from the box, he said, like oil. They wouldn't hurt me. They were merciful creatures. They'd find the apiary on their own.

"And they're safe to transport in a box, in the back of a van?"

Yes, of course. He regularly drove around with a carful of bees.

After I thanked him for his time and he said goodbye, his phone hovered in its receiver, and I could hear him whispering tender words he thought no one else could hear: "Oh, darling. You can have my waffles. Yeah. You like that?" By the time I rushed to hang up, I was all red with the hot shame of happening, uninvited, upon an intimacy not my own.

I counted my allowance and came up with enough for four pounds of bees. I wanted it to be a surprise for Tim Gary. But when I went to ask Therese for the keys to the bus, she was sitting with him in the kitchen. She gave me the key and asked, "Where are you going?"

I hesitated. I said, "I have to run an errand."

On her face I saw something distrustful. She asked me to pick up skim milk.

The parish printer was out of ink, so I'd written the directions on both sides of a napkin. I took the turnpike out of town, and the van lurched and pitched as I charged into Massachusetts.

I ate graham crackers straight from the sleeve. Mine was the only vehicle on the road, and there were no houses, just blank pasture, until I turned off the paved street and onto a long driveway of gravel and dust.

I thought, at first, that I'd arrived at the wrong house—I saw no beehives in the yard, no man traipsing around in a white suit. Just the low, wide house of clapboard siding, the windows covered with sun-leeched sheets of newspaper. An awfully dark place to be breeding bees, I thought. I checked the house number against what I'd written down, then turned off the ignition.

The apiarist had bushes of raspberries near the road, the fruit gone squat and hard. The grass was frosted with dandelion heads; I bent to stroke it. In the treeless yard, a low plastic pool with dregs of rotten leaves, and on the porch a paint-stripped bike thrown on its side.

At the door, I heard them first: the drone like a quivering siren, a maddening thrum. And then the apiarist opened the door and I stared: bees. Hundreds of them. They clouded the air, diving and climbing with ease around the front room. They looked like they were floating, and seemed almost beautiful, until I remembered I was afraid.

From a metal jug, the apiarist—there he was in front of me, bald and gaunt and wearing an undershirt—shot smoke in the air, and the bees slowed as if in obeisance. A few drifted past me through the open doorway and I jerked with fright.

His little arms were so pale they looked gray, and thick chest hair poked up from the neck of his yellow shirt. As he spoke, I watched a bee hover and lower itself onto his nose. "It's not every day I get a visit from a bride of Christ," he said. He seemed delighted by my habit and veil. He smiled dopily, displaying only a half mouthful of teeth, and stepped aside to

202

let me in. "These weren't raised to be God-fearing bees, I'm afraid."

The room was floored in linoleum, walled with slats of dark imitation wood, and empty except for a low-hanging light bulb and a white wooden beehive, uncovered. And, of course, except for the bees. They made the air seem foggy, almost viscous. Crowds of them danced over the surface of the hive. Others rose and sank and came to rest on the wooden frames bordering the windows, or on the apiarist's shoulders and head. The rest were set on soaring. They approached me with interest and I shut my mouth. I dug my nails into my own forearm.

The apiarist asked what he could do for me.

"I called earlier," I said. "About the Carniolans."

He nodded and gestured for me to follow him to the back of the house, where the bare hallway gave way to a wide room with a narrow striped mattress, a brown blood spot in its center. He must have slept among these bees, dozed to their thrum.

With his back turned, he rifled in a dark closet, and he couldn't see me standing frozen, trying to appear inanimate so the bees might pass me by. It was beyond my understanding, that Tim Gary might find this a pleasant way to spend his time.

Crouching low, the apiarist assembled a cardboard box. With his bare hands he lowered a hunk of comb, bees clinging fast, into the box. I watched him slowly tip the box up over itself so it lay flat on a white sheet, and then he propped up a corner with a two-by-four. "Now they'll tell their friends how nice it is inside the box," he said. I watched the bees wander in and out, as if making up their minds. "In, oh, half an hour or so, we'll have a good four pounds of bees in there."

I nodded. I didn't ask: How many bees to the pound?

In the kitchen he served me a bottle of cola. He offered me pickle spears fingered from a wide-neck jar. I shook my head.

The apiarist ate his pickles with loud snaps. Through the back door a dog came panting—a rib-thin, bear-faced dog. His walk seemed to hurt him, but he delighted in the presence of water in his bowl, in the hands of the apiarist digging through his ratty fur.

"Freddie boy," the apiarist cooed, crouching to kiss the dog's wet nose. "That's my Freddie." He turned to me. "You can pet him, if you like."

I knelt down to meet the dog's face, and he breathed at me, hot and hard. Bees latched to the dog's tucked belly and greasy ears, but Freddie never stopped to swat or shake them free.

"He likes you," the apiarist said.

I smiled.

"Are you looking at his balls?" he said. I wasn't, but then I saw them and could not ignore them. Bulbous, fat. The healthiest part of him.

"Oh, I'm sorry," the apiarist said. He scratched his nose with a wet finger. "'Balls' is a swear, isn't it?"

"No, no, don't worry," I said. I sat on the floor at Freddie's flank and watched him lick freely at the water in his bowl, though several dead bees floated on the surface. He was the kind of trusting dog who seemed not to know how bad things were.

When I stood back up, I saw that a bee had drowned in my cola and come to rest on the surface. I poured the pop down the sink and picked the bee from the drain.

The apiarist sighed and pointed to the trash can. He told me things had been lousy for him and his bees that winter. His population had been cut in half. Lately, his queens were laying fewer eggs. "One thing about queens," he said, "they don't like to be helped along. They like it to be their idea, if you know what I mean."

I set my bottle on the counter—a tiny clink.

"Say, Sister," the apiarist said. "How about you help me with something in the garage?"

His garage was detached from the house, with a wide square-faced pull-down door gaping a foot. He unlocked the side door, and Freddie rushed in first.

There was no car or truck, only amassed disorder. Eight feet of an artificial Christmas garland, studded with imitation pinecones. Towers of thick, glossy science fiction novels. A tower of canned beans and corn. A woodworking bench and low table saw, an upended electric keyboard, a dozen empty tissue boxes, a microwave.

I waded in. Freddie's tail upset a crate of empty amber prescription bottles, and they went flying. But the apiarist ignored him. He perched a foot on the arm of a rusted lawn chair, stretched back so I could see the bulge of his groin. He said, "This is my little hideout. My little sanctuary." When I didn't say anything, he looked hard at my face, then grinned. "Well. It beats me why a pretty girl like you would be interested in the clergy."

I spoke, my voice unsteady. "You said you needed my help?"

"See, I'm having trouble with that old door. It won't go down the whole way. And I get a draft. Then little critters come in at night. Damn mice that come and nest in my easy chair." He gestured to an armchair that had been busted, its fluff ripped free.

I looked at the gaping door, the foot of liminal space, the threshold for escape.

"I'm sure I won't be much use," I said, arms crossed. "I'm no stronger than you."

The apiarist walked over and tugged on the strap hanging from the door. "It just won't give! I don't know. It's jammed, maybe, or rusted stuck."

By then Freddie was sniffing my leg, and I thought the apiarist wouldn't see me slip a piece of graham cracker from my purse. I thought, from where he stood, he couldn't see me let Freddie lick the crumbs off my palm. But Freddie ate with loud smacks of his tongue, and the apiarist flung around and stared hard at my outstretched hand.

He raised his voice then, rage swelling in his face. "You. Do. Not. Feed my dog. Without. My. Permission."

"I—I was just—"

The apiarist's eyes went wild. For a second it seemed he would come at me. I was done for, I thought. This was it. I could see it all unfold: the violent lunge, my futile attempt to run. My body tied up and the story on the nightly news. But instead he called Freddie over to his side and stuck his hand inside the dog's mouth. He scraped gummy bits of cracker from his teeth and pink tongue. Freddie's eyes went shut, and he whined from somewhere deep within. I watched the man rake the dog's throat with one hand and hold his head with the other. Later, I'd recall the look on his face: there was, for a moment, unprecedented tenderness, as if his dog was owed every last store of his love.

Maybe I'd only imagined the danger of being in a small space with this strange man; maybe he had no wicked intentions. But right then I permitted myself the right to see my fear as proof enough. I collected myself, and then, while the man's hand was still between the jaws of the dog, I fled. I rushed out the side door.

In the van, I hurried the engine awake and punched the gas and leapt the curb and started to soar. And even without the bees, I was feeling good, so good—feeling all sorts of brave and a variety of stupid and a certain kind of lucky, the kind that comes after you circumscribe danger with your own will and good sense. The wind welcomed me to newfound speed. I smiled out the windows at fields of erect trees.

I didn't want to go home. I drove down every street I could. I went over the bridge and then turned around and drove back the other way. Past the wind turbines and the movie theater and the strip club with the all-you-can-eat breakfast buffet. I kept reminding myself that I would eventually have to turn the van toward home, but then when it was time to make the next turn, I would forget. Or maybe it was more willful than that. It was so easy to keep turning down the wrong streets.

When I finally did return home, Therese was mad: I forgot to pick up milk.

66.

The third weekend of March, Therese organized the opening of a swap store in downtown Woonsocket, in the old shoe repair shop. The swap store was intended to be a store without money, just things. Above and beyond capitalism. People were welcome to bring goods and trade, or bring nothing and take. It was all Therese's idea—help people get rid of their old junk, and help other people find stuff they might need. The others worked with her to spread the word and make sure no one tried to trade anything illegal.

I went with Tim Gary that first weekend. He wanted to get there before the good stuff was claimed. In the swap store, Frances had hoped to find a twelve-quart Crock-Pot for beef stew. Tim Gary wanted a new belt, an extension cord, a reading lamp.

The shop was crowded, and it smelled like dust and rot, like things forgotten, even though everything had just been unpacked. The room was no bigger than a two-car garage, lit by a single light bulb hanging from the ceiling. People were set on finding treasures. They rifled through DVDs and sank their hands into bins of costume jewelry. They flipped through tapes labeled ADULT. They made the dishes clink. They raked hanging frocks and blouses along the rack. There was a disproportionate number of hammers. Whole buckets of them. A table was stacked with abandoned toiletries: half-empty bottles of shampoo and lotion, pumps poised like the necks of hungry birds. Pots and pans still barnacled with grime. Near the front there was a whole table full of religious paraphernalia: porcelain cross-shaped keepsake boxes, little baptismal gowns and First Communion dresses, and Bibles. Tons and tons of Bibles.

Piled on top of each other, these things didn't seem so desirable, but still people paced, picking up pieces of junk and turning them around in the air.

Then I turned to see Lawnmower Jill among the free weights in the front corner.

We smiled at each other. I asked her if she was trying to get buff, and she said she was. She looked at her watch and told me she was also sixty-one hours sober. She'd been kicked out of Getchell House a couple of months back, and now was living in public housing across the river. She had a job, making submarine sandwiches. She was trying to be good.

"Good," I said.

But Lawnmower Jill heard a question. "Yeah, good—you know. Clean, well-behaved. A real upright citizen. Yada yada yada."

She did look clean. Her parka was still missing squares of fill, but it looked recently laundered. Her hair was washed and stuffed in a braid, her fingernails trimmed close.

I told her I was proud of her. I asked her what she'd been leaning on to help her keep upright.

"Oh, I don't know. Most days, myself."

I nodded. We were quiet for a moment. "And how is Horse?" I said.

She got this sad look, as if her face was too heavy for her head. "Locked up. County." She got picked up stealing a microwave hamburger from a gas station, and she had enough heroin on her, Lawnmower Jill said, "to sink an oil rig."

I said I'd be sure to write Horse a letter. And I did write

Horse a letter, telling her I missed her, and I included the funnies from the paper. But then I couldn't remember what her real name was, when I went to address the envelope. I had to call Abbess Paracleta: it's Eleanor.

Lawnmower Jill said, "I always liked you, Agatha." She studied my face. "You're not like the other sisters."

I would think about that comment for years.

67.

That week I taught my students the Pythagorean theorem, but I spent the most time talking about what I'd learned online, when I'd searched "Pythagorean theorem please help." According to legend, after Pythagoras discovered his famous theorem, he was so high on his own genius, he killed one hundred oxen in celebration. There was a word for sacrificing a hundred oxen: it was called a hecatomb. "Say it with me," I said, to my students. "Hecatomb. Hecatomb. Hecatomb."

When I came home from school, there was newspaper spread over the kitchen floor, swaths of my sisters' hair atop it.

"We had a slow afternoon," Mary Lucille said, and pulled off her veil to show me. "Therese cut mine. Do you like it? See how she angled the bangs?" She studied my face. "I can cut yours, too, if you want."

"That's okay," I said. I felt useless, and pathetic, and I hated both these feelings, and then I hated myself for feeling them.

Father Steve gave me pamphlets to distribute to my students about religious life. He'd designed them himself, he said. The front read "Vocation: All I Ever Wanted!" and there was a photo of a few nuns laughing. What was so funny, I wanted to know.

Inside, the text was very small and squished onto both sides of the paper. I read it alone at my desk. "How do I know if I'm being called? Your journey starts with discernment. Very few

people regret listening to God's call. You only have one life—
why not give yours to God?"

I put the pamphlets in a low desk drawer. If girls came to me
and asked for advice about becoming a sister, I'd have something to give them. But they never did.

68.

Easter was cold and gray. On the kitchen table we left chocolate bunnies for Tim Gary and Baby and Pete and Eileen, and then we spent the day the way we spend every Easter: solemnly. From dawn to dusk we sat in metal folding chairs in the parish, thumbing rosary beads, praying the glorious mysteries again and again.

There were times when I did not stop at Amen. I could make the Beatitudes go on and on. There was never enough time to list all the blessed. Blessed are my students, I said, and blessed be their friends; blessed are the quitters; blessed are the nervous; blessed are those who hide; blessed are the messy; blessed are the ones who say "Oh, that's over my head"; blessed are the late bloomers, and blessed are the foolish; blessed are those who lisp; blessed are the birthday party clowns; blessed are the waitresses; blessed are the awkward; blessed are those who burn the roofs of their mouths because they cannot stand to wait; and blessed are the heartbroken, the ones who haven't arrived at the other side of their pain. Thank you very much. Amen, amen, amen.

For as long as I could remember, Easter had never been happy. Easter was when there was blood on the rug. Easter was when I was sent next door to be with the neighbor while my mother was driven to the hospital to die.

My father told me how it happened. He said it had to do with her womb. My mother had had a difficult time delivering me—thirty hours of labor and then a C-section—and after I was born, she asked a doctor to place one of those copper devices in her uterus so another baby wouldn't be conceived.

For years, she sat in the confession box and listed sins: she'd raised her voice to my father, parked illegally, envied the women in magazines, missed credit card payments, drank too many glasses of wine. She'd honked her horn, picked the neighbor's forsythia for herself, muttered swears when she nicked herself shaving, cursed God when she shrank a sweater in the wash. She prayed a dozen prayers, doubled her penance, but it wasn't enough: still she suspected it was wrong to have the copper inside her.

And a priest told her she was right: it was a sin to keep a baby from being made, from being born.

She conceived my brother a month after the device was removed. I was eleven, and witnessed crying jags that lasted hours. I remember her vomit. Her swollen ankles. There were afternoons I'd watch her stand at the mailbox and look down the street for what seemed ages, or sit in her parked car awhile before she came in the house.

My baby brother was born a month early to a mother who hemorrhaged in the bath on Holy Saturday. I remember the siren, and sitting for hours in the next-door neighbor's TV room while she smoked in the kitchen. And I've tried to forget, but I can picture so clearly, still, the way my father's face looked when he came home on Easter with a baby and no mother.

For Easter dinner, Mary Lucille planned to make lamb like Mother Roberta taught her. The Easter before, she had cooked a rack of lamb studded with peppercorns and served with mint jelly. And so in Woonsocket Mary Lucille went and bought a heavy hunk of meat, wrapped in white paper. But she forgot to pick up mint jelly, so when we left the church together after our last rosary, I told the others I'd stop by the Price Rite and meet them at home. The humidity had lifted, and I walked along Hamlet Avenue feeling light.

Woonsocket's water used to be kept in a tower on Hamlet, one of those great steel orbs standing on four legs in the sky. It was stationed between the church and town, rusted over and empty. Back in the seventies, they put a light up top so planes wouldn't nick the orb and flood the town.

The light also made it so that I could see Tim Gary climbing up the water tower's caged ladder. I knew him by his tiny frame and the shape of his hair from the back.

That night I never did pick up a package of Sure-Jell or a bunch of mint leaves. I came home a couple of hours later, with Tim Gary, empty-handed and hungry. The others had cooked the lamb and the leftovers had cooled, and they were indignant, hands on their hips—where had we been? And why was I covered in mud?

I fell, I said, and I had: I slipped twice, running to him across wet grass, and there was mud all down my front. By the time I got to the bottom of the ladder, he was thirty feet up, ascending at a steady clip.

"Tim Gary!" I called.

He looked down. It seemed to take him a second to remember who I was.

"What're you doing?" I yelled.

"Huh?"

"What! Are! You! Doing!"

He didn't answer. He turned back to the ladder, and I climbed up to meet him. The rungs of the ladder were muddy where

215

he'd stepped, but I didn't care. I held tight and lifted one foot at a time. When I reached the steel platform, I hauled myself up and sat next to him.

"I didn't know you could climb like that," Tim Gary said.

"Me neither," I said. I was out of breath.

We sat facing all of Woonsocket, lit up by streetlamps and other people's porch lights, and Tim Gary swung his legs and told me how things used to be. A century ago, on the other side of the river, there'd been rubber and textile mills, back when those were industries on which you could build a town. Last he knew, most of the mills were condominiums now. And there used to be a pizza-by-the-slice place he loved, just beyond the trees, near where he had lived with his ex-wife. Now it was a dry cleaner's.

It made me smile to picture a younger Tim Gary, with more hair and more muscle and a whole jaw, a napkin tucked in his collar and a slice of pizza propped up in front of his face. But then this also made me sad.

Off to the east beyond the evergreens I could see the very top of the turbines, so that when each blade rose up I caught just a glimpse before it sank again.

"What was it like?" I asked. "Living alone, I mean. After— when you—"

"After my wife left?" he said, and I nodded.

Back then, his loneliness was enough to rot a bag of sugar. He told me he fell in love with anyone who asked him how his day was going. After his surgery he drove himself to the mouth doctor and the cancer doctor and the bone doctor, and when he left he wanted so sorely to tell someone whatever it was the doctors had said. "I tried to tell the checkout boy at the hardware store," he said, "but it was not as interesting to him as I hoped." It was all Tim Gary could do each day to go stand

216

among the wrenches and work at being alone. He had never learned how not to need someone.

"At the doctor's, I kept getting good news," he said. "And I was supposed to be happy. But can I tell you something?" I watched him try to find a way to say it. "Ever since then—"

I waited.

"It's not that it's any one thing—" He sighed. "Well. It's just. I don't think I have the constitution for it. For being alive."

He turned to look at me. I touched his shoulder. There were ways, I knew, to tide a man over. My sisters were very skilled at steering unhappy men toward God. They could give a man a why.

But whys can leak from you, I knew. You couldn't help it. You had hope, and then it slipped away. You belonged somewhere, and then you didn't.

"Yeah," I told him. "I understand."

"I wonder if I'll be any better at being dead."

I didn't know what to say to this. "When the time comes, I think you're going to be a smash hit in heaven," I said after a moment. "A household name."

He smiled.

"But not for a long time," I added. "You've got to stick around. Don't you want to find out what else they'll build in Woonsocket?"

"Condominiums," he said.

"Condominiums," I agreed.

He said, not unkindly, "You know, you're lucky, Agatha, to have them. Frances and Therese and Mary Lucille."

I nodded; I knew that this had once been true. I've never be able to explain, even to myself, why it couldn't be made true again.

I worked my throat and leaned to spit a loogie onto the

217

grass below. I could watch it drop part of the way, but it disappeared in the dark and I couldn't see where it landed. After a moment Tim Gary spat, too. It didn't feel like catharsis, but it was something to do.

I pointed east across the field and asked Tim Gary if he could see the turbines beyond the trees. He couldn't make them out, so I pointed and said, "There, right there," and he stared hard and said, "Where?" and "Where?" and then, "Oh, oh!"

We sat, quiet, and watched the blades slice the night. I knew Tim Gary was waiting for me to speak, but I couldn't come up with a pithy moral to impart. It took me months to figure out what I should have said, and longer to forgive myself for not saying it: when it comes to purpose or meaning or reasons to live, all we can hope for is something akin to that "Oh, oh!"

I tried to count the turns of the moonlit blades, but the longer I looked, the more one blurred into the next, and I lost track and gave up. Or I gave up and then lost track; I'm not sure which.

PART III

OBEDIENCE

69.

There was much I could not control, and among these things were allergens: dust and ragweed and grass. Also, pollen. Woonsocket's air was crummy with pollen. I shot my nasal cavity with saline, watched it drip out the other side. At night I propped my pillows up so I could breathe.

And then one night I felt a hair on my chin.

I switched on the light and made everyone else come close to stroke it. I was worried I was imagining it, but they confirmed that yes, one dark, wiry hair had arrived.

It was as if all my life had been leading to the growth of this little hair. But after the joy, guilt rushed in: I hadn't spoken to Mother Roberta in months. This wasn't for lack of a telephone or time or desire—I thought of her often, yes, and wondered how she was, even thought to call her, but hadn't. I was busy, and tired.

We called Mother Roberta in the morning, all of us staring at the speakerphone.

We were patched through. When she came to the phone, she said, "This is Roberta."

My heart swelled. The sound of her voice, the delight in her tone—it was like being reintroduced to myself. The overhead light seemed warmer, the walls less far away.

"I'm sorry I haven't called. I should have," she said to us. "I'm sure you've heard the news by now."

"What news," I said.

"My jubilee," she said. "It's going to be my Golden Jubilee."

Mother Roberta had given fifty years to the church. She had

watched the rise of a half-dozen popes and too many bishops. She'd witnessed the turmoil of Vatican II. For decades she had watched as men she knew, men of holy devotion, men who counseled others in matters of faith, were revealed to be stupid or depraved. She had prayed a million rosaries, mentored a thousand young religious sisters. Fifty trips around the sun. More than eighteen thousand days.

"They're throwing me a party," she said. "Here at the home. They insisted. There'll be a Mass, and a potluck."

Mary Lucille said, "How special! How nice."

"Say you'll come," she said. "Come home and visit."

"Oh, I don't know," Therese said. "It's a long trip."

The four of us were looking at the phone and not at each other. But when she said, "I'm getting old," we glanced up, and all our hesitation was eclipsed by guilt. I could imagine her with the portable phone, vulnerable on the couch: the tiny arms and the slump of her shoulders, the kinked fingers, the bulbs of her knuckles.

Frances told her we'd be there. I felt a surge of joy: it might be nice for the four of us to journey somewhere together, the way we used to. I wanted us to return to Mother Roberta and be able to say we had been loyal and loving, so at the end of her life, when she looked down from her seat at the heavenly dais and listed the people on earth she most wanted to join her in heaven, our names would be among the first.

We called the abbess and asked if she was willing to come stay at Little Neon while we drove to Lackawanna. She said yes, but for three days only, and we were not permitted to use the white van for non-Neon-related travel.

And so, the week after Easter, we rented a car. Our first

time, and we were plainly thrilled. For forty-three dollars plus the price of gas, we had a car wide as a ship. It was far fancier and cleaner and quieter than the big white van or the red Mercury Villager we'd driven in Lackawanna. This was a blue four-door sedan, with plush interior and an air conditioner that we put on full blast without a second thought. Everything about the car was beautiful: the glint of the trunk, the dashboard's slope, the sound of the lock.

"What kind of engine?" Therese asked the rental car agent. He wore a green vest and looked bored.

"Big one," he said.

When Frances told him how excited we were, to be heading to our dear friend's jubilee in this beautiful car, he said, "Yeah. Here's the keys."

We piled in, and Therese started it up. "Oh, man. Listen to her—"

"We know, we know," Mary Lucille said. "Listen to her purr."

In the days before our trip, the four of us mentioned the jubilee in every conversation we had. At school I told my students I'd be gone for a couple of days, and they'd have a substitute, because I would be out of town, attending my dear friend's jubilee. They were expected to be well-behaved and keep up with their assignments while I was at my dear friend's jubilee. I'd collect their homework after I got back from my dear friend's jubilee.

At the dinner table, the Neons grew tired of hearing about it. They stared at the wall while we talked. Over goulash we speculated about what food might be at our dear friend's jubilee. Washing the dishes, we hoped for fine weather for our dear friend's jubilee. Oh, on the way to our dear friend's jubilee, we'd have to stop at the fishmonger's in Lackawanna to pick up blue crab to bring to the potluck that would follow our dear friend's jubilee.

"Sisters," Pete said, his eyes like bullets. "Please. Enough about the jubilee."

My head continued to hum with excitement. It had been many months since I'd seen Mother Roberta flash those gleaming false teeth. I could still picture her smile, and the brackish blue skin on the tops of her hands. But I'd forgotten the precise slump of her back, the way she looked me in the eye.

I shuddered to picture the way Father Thaddeus's belly pushed against his shirt, the wispy hairs atop his head.

The night before the trip, I gathered my cold cream and toothpaste and nasal decongestant spray. I slipped nylons and pairs of underwear into a duffel bag. And then, kneeling next to the others, I joined them in prayer. We prayed for the abbess and Tim Gary and Pete and Eileen and Baby and my students and the substitute, and we prayed for Horse and Lawnmower Jill, and then we asked for a safe trip, and fine weather, no trouble from the car. And we asked that this weekend Mother Roberta might feel like no one was missing and nothing was out of place.

While the others slept, I heard noise downstairs. I went down in my nightgown and found Tim Gary at the kitchen table, drinking apple juice and listening to a handheld radio. When he saw me in the doorway, he sat up straight and switched the radio off.

"Sorry—was it too loud?" he said.

I said no, I just wondered what the sound was. He told me

he'd found it at the swap store and given up his headphones for it. "Now that guy has headphones but no radio, and I have a radio but no headphones," he said. He knew it was old-fashioned, but he liked to listen to the requests and dedications on the easy-listening channel.

He switched it back on, and we waited for the song to end. Then DJ Shezeen let us know that the next song was a request from Maisie. "This one is for Maisie's true love, Ridge. Ridge, Maisie's thinking of you and missing you from all the way in sunny Santa Barbara. She wants you to know she's coming home to you soon." The song started, and I didn't recognize it.

I asked Tim Gary if he would be all right while we were away, and he said he'd be busy with work. "But I have some videotapes I've been meaning to watch, and I might walk down to the tire and back. Maybe Pete will want to join." He smiled at me.

That sounds nice, I said. I was eager for reassurance that he'd be all right, and this was enough.

The next request was from someone named PJ. He wanted it to go out to his roommate. "Danny, if you're listening, PJ wants you to please stop and pick up trash bags on your way home. He would like it if they were the kind with the draw-string."

70.

We left at dawn in our sleek blue car as soon as the abbess showed up. She told us to drive safely and asked where we would be staying, in case she needed to call us. The Super 8, Therese said, and then she got behind the wheel and we were flying out of the driveway, and soon we were on the interstate, speeding ahead. The thrill of the open road! I pressed my face to the window and watched the world pass us by.

On our way out of Woonsocket, we passed the wind turbines, and Therese slowed down in the right lane so we could look. In all our time in Woonsocket, I'd never seen the turbines look so big and graceful. How proud they looked! I should have asked Tim Gary how it worked, how the wind could be turned into something else while the turbines stayed in place.

Therese drove for many hours. She clucked her tongue at slow-moving vehicles. In Massachusetts, we stopped for lunch. We'd packed provisions: cold sausages in cans and hot coffee from a thermos. Someone distributed wedges of an orange.

At a picnic table across the parking lot sat a group of boys in scouting vests. They were slumped over their lunches, and they made no noise. A fat one stood and walked to the toilets; when he was gone, the others broke into whispers and jeers. Uneasy, we watched them snicker to each other, and knew without hearing that they were mocking him when they had the chance. When the fat one came back to the table, the boys returned to their boxes of juice, a great play of innocence.

Then we watched the boys fill a yellow bus and go. The

jump and rattle of the engine as it hurtled on and disappeared behind the trees.

We shook our heads and wiped our hands and fastened our seatbelts. How horrible, how merciful, the ways we are, each of us, oblivious to so much of the hurt in the world.

To pass the time, we listened to public broadcasting. The news: men were murdering, sea levels were rising, deer were dying, celebrities were giving birth.

Mary Lucille and I had a thumb war, which ended in a draw after Mary Lucille issued allegations of foul play.

Therese hushed us and turned up the volume: the broadcaster was speaking about priests in another city.

"Can we please turn this off," Mary Lucille said.

It was anguish to listen to, but I felt no shock. We'd never said much to each other about the news reports, not even when we were alone in the attic. There were only ever moments of outrage that would flare out, and then we would go to bed.

Mary Lucille leaned forward from the back seat to switch it off, but Therese swatted her hand away from the dial. "To date, the Vatican has paid more then two-point-six billion dollars in settlements," the broadcaster said.

"Two billion dollars," Frances said, eyes wide. "Oh, this is so much worse than I thought."

"Oh, I don't like listening to this stuff," Mary Lucille said. "Turn it off."

"Turning it off won't help," Therese said.

The broadcaster listed parishes and priests. After a moment, he went to a commercial, and Therese hit the dial.

The car was silent for a painful moment, and I felt a familiar eddy start up inside me, a private countercurrent of rage. They had not imagined consequences, these priests, these men who could baptize and anoint and transubstantiate, men who could stand at the pulpit and speak of temptation, then, warped by a sense of impunity, do what they wanted in the world, including rape in the middle of the day, then sit on the other side of the confession box and listen to people list their sins. They had believed they were beyond reproach. And in a way, they were right, because for so long, nothing happened to these men. Reassignments, maybe, and resignations, but nothing like reproach.

I said, "And where is the pope in all this? Suddenly he has nothing to say?"

Frances turned to frown at me. "Agatha. Show some respect," she said.

"Agatha's right," Therese said, and she glanced at me in the rearview mirror. "What a mess these men have made."

"Oh, it's not for us to say," Mary Lucille said. "Who are we to judge?"

I suppose, for her, deference was all wrapped up with obedience. That's what the vow meant in her mind. But I was all out of deference.

In Stockbridge, we stopped for gas. When the tank was full, we pulled out onto the street, next to one of those huge trucks that looked like it could be used to invade a country. Therese had to gun it when the light turned so she could pull out ahead of the big truck and get back on the highway.

The truck driver was not pleased.

He honked like mad. He revved his engine so his headlights were inches from our bumper. We turned back to see the looming hood of the truck, close and huge. My heart raced.

This was how we would die, I thought. The man was yelling things we couldn't hear, but we watched his teeth snarl, his fist shake. He was a stocky man, with a head wider than it was tall.

On the highway he continued to tail us, so close that if Therese were to take her foot off the accelerator, the hood of his truck would be in our trunk, and our seat belts would lacerate our torsos, and we would surely die.

"Let him pass," Frances told Therese. "Pull over."

So Therese steered onto the shoulder and slowed to a stop. But then we watched in horror as the truck driver did the same and parked in front of us.

In a flash his door was open and he flung himself onto the road, charging toward us with wild eyes. Therese locked the doors. The four of us panted with fear. In the backseat Mary Lucille and I held hands tight tight tight.

We heard him yell: "You fucking cut me off again—"

We shut our eyes and started to pray an Our Father.

The man pressed his head to the driver's side window. Something about us—our habits, our lips moving with our eyes shut—made him howl with laughter, and then he pounded on the glass.

"I didn't realize you was a bunch of nuns," he yelled into the car. "I didn't mean to be a jerk. I'm sorry."

Not every one of God's creatures deserves your mercy— that was another thing Mother Roberta had taught us. You don't always have to give someone an out. We had our chance to tell the man, "Your rage is the stuff of hellfire. You're a loser, through and through. Get lost." And I did want to, safely behind glass, but then I muttered my way through the rest of the Lord's prayer with the others, until we landed on "Amen."

"I can't hear you!" the man called. "Roll the window down!"

But we only looked ahead and kept our mouths shut.

"Seriously, I had no idea," he called. He waited, and when we said nothing, he started to walk away. Before he got into his truck, he turned and gave us a smile, and said, "Hey, have a nice day! God bless."

It's my belief that many men sleep too soundly at night.

Therese let the man get a head start, then counted to one hundred and twenty and started back on the road.

We were on I-90 forever, until we weren't, and Buffalo started all at once. I had not expected the surge of nostalgia. Wistful anxiety—it came and took hold of me and didn't let go. The streets were insulated with trees, dogwoods and oaks. We crossed the Buffalo River, that puny thing. It took less than ten seconds to drive across, and we held our breath. Some people believe in holding their breath in tunnels or passing a graveyard, but that's hogwash; better, we've always agreed, to hold your breath on a bridge, lest it collapse.

Two more tedious miles, and then Lackawanna.

Everything we saw seemed at once familiar and very strange: the pharmacy, the halal butcher, the non-halal butcher, the supermarket where we used to eat bakery donuts while shopping and then forget—we swear—to pay. I didn't know what to do with all my longing.

We stopped first at Burhop's for fish.

The fishmonger, we found, had not changed one bit. He was still young, mustached. Bright eyes. A handsome smirker. "Burhop!" Frances said, her joy so palpable that for a second I thought she might reach over the counter to kiss him.

She had expected him to be surprised and happy to see us, but he did not seem to know we had ever left Lackawanna. "Sisters, how we doing," he said. "Talk to me."

This was his standard greeting, which he used with every customer. He liked to holler and joke. The things he said were colored with insincerity, flirtation. But this, we'd always tolerated, because he sold decent fish.

Or he had, once. Mary Lucille examined the fish in its case and turned to look at each of us—it was not what she remembered.

Frances agreed. Missing were the grouper and the rockfish she had loved.

"The tilapia looks too orange," Therese said. There was yellowing shrimp, dull haddock gone bloody, and flounder that had grayed.

I didn't know how to convince them that nothing had changed; this was the same fish we'd bought before. Maybe they had always liked fish more than me, or maybe their memories had glorified the conditions and colors of Burhop's seafood: they remembered salmon so tender it fell from the bone. Glassy filets, scallops like jewels. Low prices, thick cuts.

"Burhop," Frances said, desperate, confused. "The fish is not the same."

Burhop only shrugged. "Same fish, Sisters. Same Burhop."

For Mother Roberta, we wanted blue crab. She liked blue crab best. But the only crab Therese found was shelled and shredded, glopped with mayo, stuffed in tiny tubs.

Therese wanted to know if it was fresh crab meat.

He cocked his face.

"Define fresh."

Caught and brought by one of his Maryland men that morning, like it used to be, Therese told him.

"From the ocean?" he said. He laughed then, his neck wrenched back. "That's what a lot of people want," he said, arms crossed, brows high. "People who don't know fish."

Mary Lucille asked what he meant, and he said, "Look, Sisters. Sisters. I'm an honest man. I run an honest store."

He said it like we ought to come to our senses, like we ought to stop wasting his time.

"But where's this fish from, Burhop?"

"The sea."

"Which sea, Burhop?"

We waited. He was smiling, red in the face. "Look. I don't know which sea, Sisters. China, probably. Russia. I don't know. I don't ask questions. Do you ask your potato chip man about the farm the potatoes came from? The fish comes in on a truck, and I display it here in the store, and you buy it and take it home and fry it up in a pan."

We looked back at the wet meat, arranged in sloppy rows. I felt sad at how different it seemed to them, and then sad that it didn't seem different to me.

We went out the door without goodbye, without any lackluster crab. Outside I was relieved to breathe air that was without taste.

71.

We drove to the spot where the old convent had been, just to see what it'd become. We were all a bit jittery with excitement, our energy erring on the side of manic. Frances sang a sped-up version of "How Great Thou Art," the words all smashed together, making us laugh.

The convent had been turned into business suites. There was a nail salon in our kitchen and a Pilates studio where our bedroom had been. Out back, they'd paved over the grass that used to be our yard. We idled near the exit and watched a woman in slacks walk across the lot. She noticed us looking and called to us, not unkindly. "Can I help you? Are you lost?"

Therese shook her head, and raised a hand to wave, and then we pulled away.

The church was empty, save for a man cleaning the windows on a ladder. We went to find Father Thaddeus in the rectory. We recognized him by his posture: his hips had always jutted forward when he stood. He was busy dragging a paintbrush across a wide stretch of butcher paper. From the side, he looked the same: grayer around the temples, maybe. The skin of his neck more loose.

Therese said, "Father, hello. It's nice to see you."

He did not lower the brush. We watched him shape a *J* and a *U* in green paint.

Frances said, "We're so glad to be back in Lackawanna."

Father Thaddeus did not turn to acknowledge us.

Frances said, "Is Mother Roberta around?"

He did not say anything else until he had finished, of his JUBILEE, the rightmost *E*, and we waited, watching him make his crooked letters.

And then he bent to set his brush in the paint tray. He still hadn't forced his eyes to meet ours. We watched him turn to wash his hands at the sink. He said, "Mother Roberta is busy in preparation. For the jubilee." He paused and turned off the faucet, then jerked around to look at us for the first time, his eyes blank. "This weekend is Mother Roberta's Golden Jubilee, you know."

Mary Lucille said, "We know about the jubilee, Father. That's why we're here."

He licked a finger and dabbed at dripping blue. "Oh, bananas. Now I've gone and smeared it."

Frances said, "*Fa*-ther."

"Yes?" Touching up the corner of the *L* with a dish rag. He stepped back to consider his work—HAPPY JUBILEE—then reclaimed the brush and started on an *R*.

I'd never liked being near Father Thaddeus. He wasn't outwardly cruel, or power-mad, like some priests could be. But he set my nerves on end. Maybe it was his bad table manners, or the fact that he'd never cared much about getting to know us, back when we lived in Lackawanna. Or maybe it was that he sweated too much. I could never pinpoint what it was.

Therese said, "There's really no way for us to see Mother Roberta before the Mass?"

He said, "Yes. I'm sorry about that." But he said it as if it gave him pleasure.

72.

Later the four of us huddled before the motel vending machine. We wanted the cheese-flavored crisps: the ones from the top row of the vending machine. We paid for the cheese-flavored crisps, and we pressed A3 for the cheese-flavored crisps, but the cheese-flavored crisps got stuck in the coil and the bag of cheese-flavored crisps wouldn't budge, despite our kicks and punches and shoulder shoves. The bag hovered there in the space between snacks and glass. The machine sucked up another dollar, and we chose the adjacent bag of crisps—garlic and herb—with the hope that as the bag fell, it might knock free the cheese-flavored crisps. But the cheese-flavored crisps only shuddered.

In our room at the Super 8, we ate the pungent garlic crisps and played a single round of euchre sitting cross-legged on the pastel bedspreads. Therese and Frances won, but they didn't cheer or high-five. They didn't look happy at all.

Frances called 411 and wrote down the address of Mother Roberta's new home. Then the four of us went about our rituals, like we did every other night: cold cream on our cheeks and petroleum jelly on our knuckles.

We prayed the rosary twice. The words came like moans, like hurt. The day had wrenched us; I felt tired in my scalp. My fingers were unsteady in their progressions, bead to bead.

And then we switched off the light and lay to stare at the broad ceiling. Outside, the rush of the highway, which I pretended was the ocean when I closed my eyes.

"My pillow smells like an ashtray," Mary Lucille whispered.

"So turn it over," Frances said. But we all knew that wouldn't change a thing.

73.

In the morning, Therese gasped to find she had stepped on a carpet-deep pin.

The blood rushed out; she cried and yelped. Therese pressed hard on the wound, but the blood kept coming. I found myself woozy at the sight of her blood, so I waited in a chair until she had at last managed to slow the surge and bandage the wound.

Down the steps, Therese could only limp, her foot heavy with pain. But she insisted on walking without help. This could serve as a reminder, she said. She could have stepped on worse.

On the balcony she stopped the maid. The girl was folding towels, listening to headphones. She had a face too young for makeup, but her eyes were ringed with black ink.

Therese spoke, her voice thick with rage: "You ought to vacuum with more attention!"

The girl seemed only then to notice us. Lifted a headphone. "Yes?" Her helpful, expectant face, the practiced smile.

Therese pointed a finger in the woman's face and took a breath to speak. I looked at the girl: her tiny body aside the heavy cart, the mountain of towels for folding. Hers wasn't the right ear for Therese's rage. She hadn't planted the pin, hadn't taken the cheese-flavored crisps, hadn't swapped the fish at the market. None of this was her fault.

Frances said, "You're doing lovely work with the towels. God bless," and took Therese by the elbow. Therese panted with frustration as we walked to the car.

The walls of the retirement home were not the color of mayonnaise. They were wallpapered. In the entryway, big, floppy flowers the size of my head.

"Is every room wallpapered?" I asked the receptionist. "In the whole house?"

Her face made no mystery of how strange she found this question. "Yes," she said.

She told us Mother Roberta was napping. "The medication she's on for her arthritis," she said, "makes her very sleepy."

We hadn't known she'd started taking medication.

"Have her hands gotten much worse?" Therese asked.

"Worse than what?"

"Than before."

"Well, they're better now that she's taking medication." The woman sounded irritated. She uncapped a marker and asked us our names, so she could make us name tags.

"Oh, no need," Mary Lucille said. "Mother Roberta knows our names."

She peeled away the cellophane backs.

"All guests have to wear them," she said. "How long have you known Mother Roberta?"

Forever, I said. Forever.

74.

Mass was celebrated in the basilica: our old, magnificent church with the vaulted hall and deep domed apse. Everything was as grandiose as I remembered it. It occurred to me that I had missed, while we were away, the basilica's exquisite ceiling, painted with illustrations of the sacred mysteries: scenes set on a background of blue, rendered with such precision I could identify the whites of the Virgin Mary's eyes. It was a wonder, the kind of art that makes you feel as if you're hovering above the earth.

Therese claimed us a pew up front in the nave. The church had ordered baskets of daisies to put everywhere, and Father Thaddeus had hung his sign on the front of the altar. It appeared he had run out of space while painting: HAPPY JUBILEE MOTHER ROBERTA, it said, the letters of her name all crammed together.

The place was buzzing: more packed than we had ever seen it. I scanned the rows; the crowd was thick with families I recognized and many I didn't, from the parish and the school and the town. The church echoed with chatter. Upset babies, ill-mannered kids fussing in button-up shirts.

When the organ struck up, I turned and leaned out to peer down the aisle at the procession: Father Thaddeus came first in a robe of white. Then a child struggling to bear the great oak crucifix, as tall as he. Next the deacon didn't proceed so much as saunter, his face jolly and upturned, as if all these people had come for him.

And then came Mother Roberta. Mother Roberta, solemn and serene. But she wasn't upright. Mother Roberta was being wheeled. We looked at each other, then back at her. She was a fraction of the Mother Roberta we remembered. Her hands were gnarled and bent, her cheeks hollow, her hair more air than anything else. She was tiny and kinked up. It looked like every heartbeat brought her pain. We'd been gone ten months, and she'd become half herself.

Still we summoned our joy and waved and smiled as she passed, but Mother Roberta did not look up. She kept her eyes forward, focused on the altar.

The aide wheeling her, some pale young thing with loving eyes—she walked with good posture and a little bit too much confidence, her smile a bit too bright. She seemed perfectly competent, as if she'd been right about everything her whole life, but of course she'd never love Mother Roberta as much as I did.

75.

After Mass the basilica parking lot was thrumming with life. We could barely make our way to the food table.

A feast had been assembled and abandoned in the sun. The rolled-up meats on the deli tray had become slick and limp, and the sliced cheese shone with oil. Browning fruits, chopped and mixed; deviled eggs, the devil melted thin; cans of pop floating belly-up in iceless water. I recognized the tray Father Thaddeus bought for occasions like this: vegetables sliced into neat rectangles, arranged around a tub of thick white dip.

I snapped open a Coke. "Warm," I reported. I slopped bits of everything onto my plate, then went to sit with the others on the steps of the parish.

I looked out: Mother Roberta, low in her chair, was surrounded by parishioners on the lawn. The God-fearers, the blessed, the repentant, toting their babies and dogs. They came and shook her hand, smiled and laughed.

It's such a blessing that I perceive only a small fraction of the world's noise. For instance, though I could, from the bottom step, see the fishmonger walking from his van in chino shorts, bearing a tub of gloppy crab, I could not hear him sing out, "Sister Roberta! Talk to me." I could not hear him speak to her as if she were a girl.

And I could see the kind way that Father Thaddeus brought Mother Roberta bottled water, and I could see that she thanked him by holding his hands in hers, but I could not hear the specific words she chose, the words that, if tender, might make me ache with envy.

After a while, the four of us rose to make our way through the crowd to Mother Roberta. I was struck, standing before her, by how collapsible she seemed. Her soupy eyes on us.

Mary Lucille said, "Mother Roberta, so nice to see you. Congratulations. Fifty years! Wow."

She raised a knobby finger to point at Mary Lucille's chest: right in front of her name tag. "Your name's got three Ls, not two," she said.

Yes, the receptionist had spelled it wrong: L-U-C-I-L-E. But then I looked too long at her pointing hand—the gnarled knuckles, fingers askew.

She saw me looking and extended her wrist, as if showing off a bracelet. She said only, "It's rheumatoid." The year before, her arthritis had been only a nuisance, something she could treat when symptoms arose. A fistful of Motrin, an ice pack every evening. But now the inflammation had won a landslide victory over her bones.

"It looks painful," I said, and when she said nothing, I went on. "Mother Roberta, it's so good to see you. I've missed you."

"Sisters," she said, to no one in particular. "I'd like some food."

To the novice standing behind her, Therese said, "We'll take her from here." The girl looked sullen, but she did not protest.

Mother Roberta only wanted vegetables from Father Thaddeus's Wegmans tray.

Frances moved carrots and celery onto Roberta's plate, then pushed a spoon through the dip and let it fall heavy on the plate.

After Mother Roberta swallowed, she said, "Oh, it's good to see you four. How have you been?"

"Been" is an ugly word for an ugly thing: the past. Days, whole strings and stretches of them, gone, with little to be proud of. Mother Roberta wanted to know how our lives were, now that we'd left the parish, but I didn't know how to sum it all up: how teaching was where I spent all my favorite hours, how I wasn't sure we were making happy people of the Neons.

When none of us volunteered anything, she spoke again. "Rhode Island's got that new windmill farm," she said. "And that river. That disgusting river."

She'd been to Woonsocket?

"I stayed a night in Providence when I was younger. In the sixties, you know, they clogged the river up with their garbage," she said. "They dammed it. Sent guys in to clear debris from the bottom. Everyone's always tossing their crap in there— love letters, pop bottles, whatever."

The four of us nodded.

She thought for a moment, then speared the last bit of zucchini with her fork, and said, "You think the water ever gets tired? Tired of going all the time."

It didn't seem like the others knew what she meant, but I nodded. Yes, the water was probably exhausted.

Later I went to the toilet and chose the stall adjacent to the handicapped. I could hear Mother Roberta and the young aide struggling. "Oh, son of a pup," said Mother Roberta, and the aide said, "Here, let me," and Mother Roberta said, hotly, "I've got it," and the aide said, "Okay."

When the three of us were at the sinks, I looked at Mother Roberta in the mirror.

"Mother Roberta," I said. "I was—do you think—I've been wanting to ask—"

I turned to face them, and the aide stared at me, but I ignored her and took a breath.

"I want to know if the questions you ask, now that you're older, are any different from the ones you asked when you were young." We looked at each other. "I want to know if you think a person asks the same questions forever."

Mother Roberta considered this. She said, "Some of the questions never change."

I nodded, trying to understand what this would mean for me.

"Agatha," she said, gently. "You can't change most of the questions. But you can always come up with another answer. Remember that."

She seemed to know something about me I hadn't yet allowed to be true.

The aide handed her a paper towel and asked her if she was ready for a slice of cake, and Mother Roberta said, "Uh-huh." They went off together, and when she was on the other side of the door, she turned back.

"I think the best you can do is pray about it," she said, "but row toward shore."

I was at a loss for words again, even though I knew that this was the last time I would see Mother Roberta: her belly full of mediocre vegetables, being led away by a woman who wasn't me.

76.

On our drive home, we spent nearly an hour on the two-lane highway behind two large trucks going the same speed, coasting side by side. We were unable to pass, and Therese grew frustrated. "Son of a scout!" she yelled out the window at some point, though of course the driver couldn't hear. She coasted on the shoulder, trying to flash her lights so the driver might see.

When one of the drivers finally pulled ahead and provided us space to pass, we soared past the trucks, unencumbered and unafraid. The sun was setting in New York, and it seemed a special sun, designed specifically for the people of the wide state, who had nothing to do but get up each morning and wait for their sun to sink below the horizon, and if they were lucky, as they were that day, the sun was generous in its light and in the colors it made of the clouds. Bright violet and pink and orange that made the sky seem to expand, and I was reminded then of the enormity of the galaxy. It was easy to forget that the universe unfolded for years and years beyond the mite of it that I could see.

The moment I wish most often I could return to, if only I were able to wade backward through the mud of time, is the split second the four of us spent together on the bridge over the Blackstone River, on the final leg of our drive, the last few miles before home. The Blackstone River's just a skinny capillary, and the bridge is only a couple of hundred feet across. But that night, when we all took a hyperbolic breath and held it, Therese switched to the rightmost lane and slowed way down so that the bridge might last a little longer, and we seemed in that moment to float above the brackish river, and the water seemed more beautiful now that we knew Mother Roberta had seen it years before, and in the dark we could not see the garbage that collected on its banks, just the shimmering spots where the water caught the moon, and we crept on, alone on the unlit bridge, and we felt our hearts throb and our faces go red, desperate as we were for air, desperate to reach the other side so we could suck fresh breaths; at the same time, though, we hoped the bridge would go on and on; it seemed we had been able, in holding our breath, to stop time; even though we knew that God only led us forward through the mud and refused to let any of us stay still, we hoped to stay forever in that car that wasn't ours, still happy and unbreathing, still unaware of all the pain awaiting us.

77.

We should have known from the newspapers: there were two newspapers on the driveway, still wrapped in blue plastic, untouched.

We should have known from the fact that Abbess Paracleta and Baby and Pete and Eileen were sitting on the front steps of Little Neon, as if they'd been waiting for us all weekend. That should have given it away.

But we didn't know. We didn't know until the abbess stood up and told us, standing outside our green house, that Tim Gary had died.

She'd tried to call us at the Motel 6, she said, probably ninety times. She'd left so many messages; hadn't the front desk passed them along?

Therese said, "Maybe, but we wouldn't know, because we weren't at the Motel 6. We were at the Super 8."

"Shoot. Six, eight—I see what I did," the abbess said.

"What happened?" Mary Lucille asked. She was already weeping. "What happened?"

Baby found him in bed in the morning, under his covers. "He was a different kind of pale. For a second I thought he was just really tired," he said. "But then I saw the puddle of throw-up. I wish I'd heard him barf, woken up sooner, done something. But he wasn't breathing." Baby didn't scream. "I didn't want to wake up the abbess, or the girls. I just woke up Pete, because he was right there."

"I'd have thought his lips would be blue," Pete said, "but they were gray. Gray like tile caulk." He told us about Tim Gary's violet hands, his arms so stiff you could snap them in half.

Pete called an ambulance. "It felt like a long time," Baby said, "waiting, after he hung up the phone." He and Pete smoked three cigarettes, standing in the street, watching for the lights of the ambulance. The siren is what woke up the abbess and Eileen, and they stared out the front window, waiting for Pete and Baby to usher the paramedics inside, which was when they found out what was wrong.

Antifreeze—for the radiator in the white van, Therese had bought antifreeze in bulk jugs the size of a suitcase. I couldn't get the image out of my head: Tim Gary in the garage, lifting the jug to pour himself a glass. All conviction, all focus. Swallowing hard to get it down. Then doing it again and again. The doctors said he drank a little less than a liter.

The paramedics came quietly, their eyes cast low. Because of the color of him, they knew not to try to resuscitate him; it was hours too late for that.

"Were they gentle," I said.

"Yeah," Pete said. "They were gentle."

But I needed to hear it again. "Were they gentle, Baby?" I said.

"Yeah," he said. "They were."

"Eileen? Were they?"

"They were."

"Abbess Paracleta?" I said. "Did you think they were gentle?"

"Yes. They were gentle."

With gloved hands they lifted Tim Gary onto a stretcher,

and then they unfolded a sheet of gauze to cover his body from head to toe. Something blistered inside me when I thought of it: his face covered up. It should have shown heavenward. I'd have pulled the gauze back, if I'd been there. A man like Tim Gary should be facing God when he left our house for the last time.

78.

I wanted to believe that Tim Gary had thought of us in the last seconds before his heart shut down, but I've since understood that what he thought was nothing at all, because his brain was the first thing to go. The doctors said his body took about six hours to shut down. He maybe had a seizure, but if he did, he didn't thrash loud enough to wake Baby or Pete. He would have sweated through his clothes, the sheets. And then there was the vomit, but he was likely unconscious by then.

And before his mind went, did he see God? Did he see someone who loved him?

The doctors couldn't answer that.

Everyone gets where they need to be, Mother Roberta had told us once. As religious sisters we were meant to surrender our needs, obey the whims of the Lord. Give it all up to God. We had no will, no command, aside from carrying out His.

We could create nothing more than a cake. All creation was left to the Father almighty, creator of heaven and earth. Ashes to ashes, dust to dust.

And death? We were meant to understand that death was not a can of soup or a type of gasoline; in other words, we could not choose it for ourselves.

For days we busied ourselves with minutiae: labeling and freezing the shepherd's pie brought by Raquelle, who worked with him at the restaurant. We had to call the morgue. We had to call the bank, the post office. No one could find the information for his ex-wife.

Abbess Paracleta had gone home to Providence the night we returned. I don't think anyone slept that night. Baby and Pete stayed all night in the living room, nose to toe on the corduroy couch; they asked to, and we couldn't say no.

And then the abbess came back the next day. To sort out details, she said. It was like the lights coming on at the end of a movie, reminding us that real life waited.

By the time Abbess Paracleta had hung up her raincoat and slipped off her clogs, Therese had microwaved a plate of shepherd's pie and filled a glass with tap water.

The abbess didn't eat her food so much as memorize it, turning it over with her fork.

She helped us arrange the wake and the funeral, and then more or less took over. She called the Bigg brothers, who ran the funeral home in Woonsocket. We'd have a luncheon after, she decided, here in Little Neon.

Frances said, "Actually, I spoke with Raquelle, and she said we could have it at the restaurant, where he worked, and they could give us—"

The abbess put up her palm. "It's not up for discussion." She seemed surprised by her own anger. Red-faced, she stood and went to scrape heavy lumps of potatoes into the trash.

79.

They buried Tim Gary on a Tuesday, before the sun got hot. The abbess organized a sixty-minute service at the church. It's customary to have a prayer service, before the body is taken from the funeral home to the church, and I told one of the Bigg brothers I'd like to lead the prayer service. A Glory Be and an Our Father and a few words about Tim Gary.

The Bigg boy had wide, frenzied eyes, and they went even wider with the idea. "That's not how it's done," he said, and shook his head, but he told me I could call the bishop and ask for special permission.

The bishop's secretary told me he was baptizing in New Haven all week, but she could try to reach him. I never heard back.

Abbess Paracleta drove us in the white van. Lawnmower Jill was already in the church when we arrived, in a pew in the back. I gave her a wave, and she started to cry. The rest of us went to sit in the front: my sisters, Baby, Pete, Eileen. I counted six people I didn't recognize in the pews between.

The bishop's eulogy startled me. He quoted the Bible in angry passages. He reviled Tim Gary for what he called "the ultimate sin: taking away the Lord's great gift of life."

In the pew I looked at my sisters with incredulous eyes. We were grieving people. He'd have done better to sing us a psalm or allow us a moment of silence.

When the others did not return my incredulity, I turned back to the bishop and set my eyes to glaring. Tim Gary was someone who loved God, who prayed and went to Mass and read the Bible and was never unkind or cruel, and he tried hard to be happy. And in turn the bishop stood behind the lectern and turned Tim Gary into not a body to be mourned, but a body to be cut up and used for parts. The stuff of a hundred Sunday homilies.

80.

I didn't know what to do with all my grief. It was mutating into fresh rage. It was becoming unseemly, teaming up with all my little disappointments to rise up and overtake me.

I had no choice but to surrender. I have loved church since childhood, back when I first knew grief, when I learned what it meant to have a mother die. Helpless me. I had no idea that the church could break your heart. I could never have imagined, in those days, a feeling big enough, strong enough, to take me from it. I could never have imagined giving up.

Sometime after Tim Gary died, I went to confession. I drew the curtain closed and kneeled and faced the metal lattice. "Bless me, Father, for I have sinned," I said.

I knew Father Steve was the one on the other side of the lattice, and I knew he would recognize me from my voice. So it took me a moment to work up the nerve to say everything I wanted to say. But when I was ready, it came without stopping. If Father Steve felt like interrupting, I never gave him the chance. And when I'd said it all, I stood and left. I didn't want to know what penance he thought I ought to do.

"My sin," I said, "or one of them, anyway, is wrath." And I spoke all my ugly anger. I listed every unfair thing. I'd given all my years to the church, I said. And now I wished I had served God some other way. I was starting to understand that Tim Gary would never walk up the driveway to Little Neon ever again. I told him that even when I was okay I wasn't okay: I was frenetic with anger. I kept looking for hope and came up only with outrage.

Maybe things would change, I said. Maybe one day the men of the church would wake up and decide to make some amendments, double back on their decrees. Maybe they'd deign to reconsider the way things worked. Surely they would, right? Someday?

But I was tired. I told Father Steve that I have looked at the world and found it wanting. The world has had women for such a long time, I said. I did not know how to be patient anymore.

81.

We women have found ways to bind ourselves to each other—floss bracelets, chain necklaces, pairs of Tops nylons. Stolen glances and eyes across the table. Donuts. Waving from windows, saving each other seats. The girls at the school liked to pass around a tube of lipstick, the most intimate thing I'd ever seen, and when it finished its loop they all had the same bright pink mouth.

We know how to mark ourselves with love, and we know how to hide away our rage. And somehow, we still exist in the world, carrying the consolation that at least we have each other.

When I left my sisters, I left with nothing.

82.

For the people who asked, I developed a script. "I found that religious life, while rich and wonderful in many ways, kept me from serving God to the best of my abilities."

People wanted an inciting incident, a chain of cause and effect, but I only gave them this single sentence; neat and serviceable and vague. I did not know what I would have said if anyone asked what my abilities were. Thank God they never did.

I thought often of one of the young nuns who'd left, years before, after hundreds of priests were accused of abuse. "What do you do with all your anger?" she asked me. We were in the laundry room, folding whites.

And I lied. I said I didn't get angry, not ever, not me.

83.

I went to live with my younger brother and his girlfriend—just a couple of weeks, I promised them, but weeks would become months would become many months. "As long as you need," he said. Each time I apologized, but I knew he meant what he said.

My little brother, Jim. My bearded little brother, Jim, who did things with computers for a living and, when he was young, liked raspberry jam and cried at the end of *Bambi*. Jim, who at four asked me if our mother was a nice lady. Who told me, after I decided to become a nun, that he'd miss me. We had always been fond of each other, but we'd never found a way to be close.

He was stiff and polite, picking me up from the Greyhound station. We remembered to hug each other, standing in front of his car.

I was back in Buffalo, sweaty and clutching a duffel bag. It was June, six weeks after Tim Gary died. The air-conditioning on the last of the three buses had not worked, and I had sweated through the crotch of my Goodwill jeans and the collar of my Goodwill shirt. I found it was easy to pass as another normal person in jeans on the bus. It was harder to know how to feel.

I didn't know if it was sorrow or relief that made me start to cry as soon as my brother shut the driver's side door and asked how my trip was.

If my brother was uncomfortable with my crying, he didn't show it. He drove without speaking and didn't ask me to explain, which I considered a mercy. Every mile we drove took me further and further from who I'd been. My throat fluttered with sobs, and when my brother merged onto the highway, the blinker was like a ticking clock.

At their apartment, I tried to be pleasant and at ease. Jules, my brother's girlfriend, guided me from room to room and spoke demurely, like a curator. There were things I saw that made me blush: the lace bra hanging from the knob on the laundry room door, the strip of photos on the fridge of them kissing, smiling, sticking out their tongues. Jules was a woman with a tiny waist and long hair. Her blouse looked like expensive silk. Every inch of her was pretty, and this made me hate the look of my Goodwill jeans, the plain sneakers I kept outside the door.

I made an effort to be neat. Each morning I reassembled the futon and folded the sheets. I kept my clothes in the hallway closet, my toothbrush under the sink. I wanted them to be able to forget I was there. So I stayed quiet. When Jules let the shower run for whole minutes while she ate a piece of toast in the kitchen, I did not remind her of the waste. Though I was tempted each time I reached for my box of oatmeal, I did not eat the chocolate-covered pretzels in the pantry. They did not belong to me.

This noisy world of rent payments and polka-dot skirts and restaurant reservations—I'd thought, years ago, that I was leaving this world for good. I had not expected I'd return.

84.

My new life brought me many firsts. I slept past twelve for the first time since I was young. I bought my first cellular phone, sent my first text message. My first time at Target: I couldn't stop finding things to admire. Glass bowls and baby clothes and tall bottles of shampoo. I bought my first portable CD player, my first CD—a band called Rilo Kiley whose album cover I liked. I bought my first pair of patent leather loafers. One Saturday, my brother made me my first gin martini, briny and cold and sharp.

Every so often my brother or Jules would ask me, not without trepidation, some question about my life before: Do you miss your routine? Were you allowed to watch television? Did you ever go bowling? Was it awful, having to wake up so early every day?

What I could never say aloud was this: that life solved so many things. I was able to postpone all my questions and inclinations. I'd solved myself for a while.

85.

I enrolled in community college. I registered for classes in sociology, calculus, French. A city bus took me to another city bus that took me right to the campus. The second bus went past the road that led to Lackawanna, and it was a relief every time the driver did not turn that way.

The French teacher was named Clarisse Patrice, which rhymed, and though I called her "Madame" to her face, I liked to say her whole name to myself. "Cluh reese puh treese." She was beautiful and young and had a blunt bob haircut. In class we learned different verb tenses, and she asked us to write about something we used to do but did not do anymore, using *l'imparfait*.

The prompt unmoored me. I stared at the chalkboard until Clarisse Patrice knelt next to me and asked if I had any questions. Did I understand the imperfect tense? I nodded. From where I sat it seemed my whole life was something I used to do but did not do anymore.

86.

I still believe that everything I have, every last butter bean and incomplete thought, is one of many ordinary blessings, something I do not deserve. I have been trying to understand what it means, to deserve. Duh serve. Dee sir vuh. I can't work out the logic of it: why I should still have what I do, when all I did was give up.

One day dovetails into the next. Some nights I am able to absolve myself. I am keen to get on with my life, and get closer to becoming someone else.

I had to write to the pope again, before I left. Nothing would be official without the Vatican's permission, Abbess Paracleta said, but she'd never seen a request denied. I met with her on a beautiful day soon after Tim Gary's funeral, before the school year was up, and through tears I told her I was ready. "And you've prayed about this?" she asked. I nodded. "And you know this won't fix anything?" I nodded again.

She had me sign a number of blank forms, all of them copies of copies of typewritten copies, the text blurry.

In my letter, I asked the pope if he remembered anything about geometry. Flip through a geometry textbook, I wrote, and you'll find lists and lists of theorems, all with diagrams for proof of the reasoning. Rock-solid logic. When I first started teaching, I told him, I looked and looked for a theorem that had been updated since the days of Plato and Euclid. I wanted to find reason to believe that the truth was amendable, that the best way to do something wasn't necessarily the way it's always done. Even when I reached the end, I went back and looked again, in case I'd missed what I was hoping for. But no: we were still using the same stuff Euclid came up with. None of the rules had changed.

It had always been the case, I told the pope, that we women were lackeys. But there was no proof or reasoning, no labeled diagram, no airtight logic to help me understand.

I signed my birth name. Abbess Paracleta told me the Holy See was very slow in confirming permission to leave. "This might take months," she said, "to be official. But you can leave now."

She told me not to tell the others; she would tell them herself. It would endanger their vocations, she said, if they knew my reasons.

I stood and shook her hand, and I thanked her, though I wasn't sure what for.

When I told the principal I was going away and wouldn't be coming back, he asked me if I had any idea how much trouble I was making. He'd have to find a long-term substitute, someone who knew math. And then start the hiring process again. Did I realize just how difficult I'd made things?

Of course, I said. Of course I do.

It was the end of the school day. The hallways were quiet and still. I closed a locker someone had forgotten to shut. In the faculty lounge I washed the coffeepot, then wet a rag and cleaned out the microwave. Things had exploded and overflowed—months' worth of slop—and no one had bothered to wipe up the mess. It didn't seem like such a hard thing to do, but only once I'd done it.

Nadia wasn't in her classroom. I thought maybe she'd already left, but her Jeep was still in the lot.

I found her in the darkroom. I knocked, and she opened the door and let me in, then shut it quickly behind me. Under the amber light, she looked drowsy and flushed. The air smelled like vinegar. The space was cramped, and I was careful not to turn or touch anything.

I asked Nadia about the film she was developing, and she said she'd photographed everything she'd thrown away in the past week. I watched her poke a print in a pan of fluid.

After a moment I told her I had to say goodbye.

"No, stick around," she said. "I'm almost done. Let's get milkshakes."

I stuck around. I waited until she'd hung the dripping sheet—the image was a toothbrush with ragged bristles—and we walked to the creamery. We ordered cookies-and-cream milkshakes and sat across from each other at a picnic table, and she started talking about a babysitter she'd had when she was young, a woman named Momo who'd made her pick up centipedes from the basement floor.

"Gross," I said. And before she could say anything else about Momo, I told her I was leaving. "The church. And the school. And Rhode Island."

She nodded. She didn't ask why. She said, "Wow," and looked into her milkshake, and then I made her promise to watch out for Samantha.

"I will," she said.

She looked at me with what I would later be sure was love.

My sisters never knew I had a friend named Nadia, or that we'd become close. All they knew was that I went to school and, hours later, came home again. I never mentioned her—not because she didn't matter, but because she did. Nadia was a marvel all my own.

When we finished our shakes, I walked her to her car. She hugged me. She kissed my cheek. And then she got into the driver's seat and shut the door. I stood there as the lights of her Jeep came on, and when she drove away I watched the rear window get smaller and smaller, until she turned a corner, and she was gone.

Four days passed. Every meal was significant to me, and every conversation with my sisters seemed a lie, a trial of withholding.

During my last dinner in Little Neon, Mary Lucille said maybe the next day we could grill corn, and I smiled. I nodded. I said, "Corn sounds nice." And then Abbess Paracleta drove me to the bus station in the middle of the night.

87.

I asked Abbess Paracleta to ship me a box of things I'd left behind—my lesson plans, my long johns, my parka.

I didn't expect a note or card, but I still looked for one. Nothing. The first-class postage was $21.17, and I mailed her back a check, as I'd promised on the phone. "Thank you so much," I wrote on a notecard, then my lapse into propriety embarrassed me, so I ripped it up and sent just the check.

My sisters were still in Little Neon. I could have called the house phone, but I never had the courage. They were waiting for another reassignment. The abbess wanted to hire someone who had experience, and they wanted to be somewhere they could be of better use.

Sometimes I allow myself to think back to our first night together, lifetimes ago. We were novices, barely passing for women before we tried to pass as women religious. We'd met at the dinner table, smiled too much. Passed the potatoes. Kept secret our anxieties. Then, in the dark, we learned the sounds of each other's sleep.

Other times, I think of the years to come, how the three of them will grow old together, will watch a hundred winters give way to a hundred springs, will pluck a thousand hairs from each other's chins. And there will be a million mornings they set the table for three and sit down together, and after a while it won't occur to them to miss me.

88.

I saw them, months later, when Mother Roberta died. She died during a snowstorm in the coldest November Lackawanna had ever seen. Abbess Paracleta told me over the phone that she got pneumonia, and then her organs shut down one by one. It was quick, she said, and Mother Roberta felt little pain.

I don't know how she found my brother's number. I sat for some time after she said goodbye, holding the receiver to my ear. I felt hollow, emptied out. I listened to the steady hum of the dial tone—the line was free and ready; I could dial anyone I wanted, someone who'd answer the phone even if their hands were full when it rang. I wanted to call the kind of friend who'd let me sob with impunity for a while, but no one came to mind.

That week, I took a bus to Lackawanna and stood in the basilica while Mother Roberta was wheeled up and down the aisle one last time—not in her chair, this time, but in a casket.

The marble floor of the church was slick and gray with tracked-in snow. There were bagpipes lamenting, a child's shriek.

Standing in the back, I was one of the last to receive Communion, to kneel and say goodbye. At the casket, I saw that the undertaker had administered a thick coat of makeup a shade too orange. But I could still see three wiry hairs on Mother Roberta's powdered chin. I leaned close and touched each of them. Her face looked proud, stoic, her eyelids shut to the beautiful dome.

There it was above me: the only untouched thing. Everything else in Lackawanna had changed, had left or died or rotted, except that blessed ceiling. As I walked to my seat, I craned my neck to look.

The mural of Mary and the angels, heavenbound—before, it had always brought me hope. But it devastated me then. I knew it was supposed to be a joyous moment for Mary, but I fixated on the details of life on earth, the palm tree behind Luke. There was a cost to salvation, I understood. I'd never considered how unbearably sad it was to have to leave so much behind.

In the pew I lowered my head and tried to pray. I didn't want to look anymore at all that great, unimaginable glory, by human minds imagined.

After Mother Roberta's casket was wheeled out of the church, Father Thaddeus and the altar boys processed back down the aisle. He would stay in Lackawanna another year, and then he'd move to Arizona. I would think of this image of him, at the front of the procession, head thrown back in pride, when, years later, I read that Buffalo priests were among the many who'd made victims of God-fearing kids.

When the procession ended I stood and slipped my arms into my parka sleeves, bent my head to try to mash together the zipper. There was to be a prayer at the gravesite, and then the parish had planned a luncheon, but I couldn't find the courage. I wanted to flee back to my brother's.

Maybe it was silly to think I could escape seeing them. During the service they'd sat up front, second pew, and from way back in the church they seemed as close to each other as ever. I'd watched them with something like contempt: the way

Mary Lucille touched Frances's back, how Frances brought her mouth close to Therese's ear. Whispering a consolation, maybe.

The teeth of my zipper would not catch, and I looked up to see the three of them coming toward me in lockstep.

I dropped the ends of the zipper and raised my eyes to face them.

Then they were there, so close I could see the dandruff on Therese's shoulders. I raised my hand to wave, and I cleared my throat to speak, but the three of them didn't see me. They were looking elsewhere. They moved past me by the time I took a breath.

89.

On the bus I sat across from a woman who looked like someone I could be friends with. She wore sensible shoes and read a novel and ate a candy bar. I smiled at her, hoping she might look up and smile back, but she didn't. At the next stop, I looked and waited for her to see me, but she continued to read. I did this again and again. Finally, she pulled the rope and stood to exit through the rear door. She walked in the direction of wherever she was going, and even when the bus went past her, I looked out the window and tried to catch her eye, and I suppose this is all I ever do: hope that despite all precedent, what I most want to happen will happen, come about and delight me.

Well. Despite all precedent, the woman did look up. She saw my face in the window. And I smiled at her, and she smiled back.

90.

"Pray," Mother Roberta had instructed me, before I left the order. One afternoon near the end, I'd called her crying. It was the first time I'd said aloud that I wanted to go. We talked only six minutes, and when I hung up, I realized I'd forgotten to ask what to pray for. But I suspect she meant forgiveness.

After her funeral, back at my brother's, I knelt sweating in front of the box fan and watched it make the curtains bloat. The blades spun at a speed I could only guess at, so fast I had no way of telling one blade from the next. On my knees, I went back in my mind to the turbines, the night Tim Gary and I sat up high on the water tower and strained our eyes to see the moonlit vanes, the red lights that blinked in the dark. Each time I revisit the memory, I imagine the turbines might take flight, lift up, go somewhere new. But then I remember that's not how they work.

It was late, and my knees hurt, but I stayed there at the window, and the blades of the fan cut the air and pushed it in my face. I shut my eyes and tried to summon the words. My God, I tried. Dear God. Oh, my God.

ACKNOWLEDGMENTS

Early drafts of this book were written when I lived nowhere, and I'm indebted to the institutions that gave me the great gifts of space and time: the National Endowment for the Arts, MacDowell, Yaddo, the Millay Colony, Lighthouse Works, Blue Mountain Center, and the Elizabeth George Foundation. Thank you to Julie Barer and Nicole Cunningham for their brilliance and conviction, and to Jenna Johnson, whose editorial acuity was invaluable. To Gretchen Achilles, Janine Barlow, June Park, Lauren Roberts, Lydia Zoells, and the entire tireless team at FSG. To Sister Sharon Erickson, for her generous insights about the lives of women religious, and to Sister Miriam Ruth Ryan. To the literary journals that published early excerpts, in different forms: *Ploughshares*, *Granta*, *Iowa Review*. At John Carroll University, thanks to George Bilgere, Anna Hocevar, Phil Metres, and Debby Rosenthal. At the University of Oregon, Jason Brown and Karen Thompson Walker. To Marjorie Celona, who provided a million varieties of support—a real superfluity. To the friends who read drafts of this book, and who have abided many hairstyles and yelled at me to bring a coat: Nicky Gonzalez, Ashley Hefnawy, Cristina Henríquez, Jim Kaberna, Ndinda Kioko, Jen Lewis, Quinn Lewis, Kate Nemetz, Asha Saluja, Alex Tanner, Leah Velez, Natalie Villacorta. To my family for your love and laughter and support: Barb, Fred, Richard, Matt, Kate, and my grandparents. Finally, to Dotun Akintoye, the brightest light, the best kind of whoa.